D0800770

FLIRTING with the Playboy

GIA STEVENS

Flirting with the Playboy: An Office Romantic Comedy by Gia Stevens

www.authorgiastevens.com

Published by: Gia Stevens

Editing by: My Notes In The Margin

Print Edition

ISBN: 978-1-958286-02-9

This is a work of fiction. Names, characters, places, and incidents either are the products of the author's imagination or are used fictitiously. Any resemblance to actual persons, living or dead, business, companies, events, or locales is entirely coincidental.

To everyone who's found love on a dating app.
This one's for you.

Blurb

Flirting with the sexy stranger on a dating app was easy. Finding out the sexy stranger is also the office playboy… I wasn't expecting that.

They don't call Bennett Pierce the office playboy for nothing. The parade of women through his doorway makes me want to dry-heave. Sure, he looks like he strolled off the page of a male fashion magazine, but his personality is anything but desirable.

But after catching my ex cheating on a dating app and Bennett witnessing my very public break up, his offer of margaritas is too hard to pass up. Tequila didn't make my clothes fall off, but it did lead to one scorching hot kiss.

Instantly, I regret it but an unexpected message on the dating app distracts me from too much self-loathing. And when the friendly banter quickly turns into steamy flirting, Bennett Pierce is one swipe right forgotten.

And when we finally meet, I realize…
I've been flirting with the playboy.

CHAPTER ONE

Cupcakes make everything better

Charlie

"Charlie."

A whisper yell sounds from my left. I do everything in my power to ignore it but deep down I know it won't stop until I give her my undivided attention. My eyes gloss over the same sentence on the computer screen for the fifth time. I don't need to read this email. If everyone misses their meetings this week, it's not my fault because it's all irrelevant compared to what's happening next to me.

"Charlie."

The voice is slightly more demanding this time. A pencil zips past my face, almost spearing my nose. My eyes follow its path as it glides to a halt on the opposite side of my desk. I slowly rotate my chair toward the direction the wooden weapon originated. Olivia, my best friend, is staring at me, eyes wide, and not so discreetly nodding her head toward the front double glass doors. We both work reception at The Blue Stone Group, Harbor Highlands largest real estate and development firm. With the city's population just shy of one-hundred thousand people, it makes it large enough that you don't see the same people twice in one day but small enough that people can and will get in your business. Sometimes referred to as a mini–San Francisco, Harbor Highlands sits on a steep hill nestled along the shore of Lake Superior and is a place I've called home for the past ten years.

My gaze follows the line of her nodding as my heart rate speeds up pounding in my throat. My hands become instantly clammy. Starting at his tobacco-colored Paul Evans loafers, my eyes drift upward over his Tom Ford navy two-piece suit, his chiseled jawline, and finally rest on his perfectly styled brown locks.

"God, that man knows how to fill a suit." Olivia's voice pulls me from my shameless gawking to see she's nibbling on the cap of her pen. I'm waiting for her to crawl over this desk and pounce on the man. Lucky for him, she doesn't.

"Earth to Olivia. You're drooling."

"I am not." She wipes the imaginary drool at the corners of her lips. "If I were you, I would follow him up to his office, tear off his clothes, and let him ravish me on his desk. Let him..."

Grabbing the same pencil she threw at me, I hurl it back in her direction, cutting her off before she goes into any more detail. "Well, for one, I have a boyfriend. And two, that man is such a condescending ass. Sure, he looks like a walking GQ ad, but when there is zero personality—I'll pass. But you should go for it." I shrug my shoulder, feigning indifference.

She pouts her lips while she thinks about it for a brief second before responding. "Nah, he's not my type. Just fun to look at." But then like the flip of a switch, excitement gleams in her eyes. "Psst, hot, condescending ass coming this way."

While trying to be inconspicuous, I peer at him through my peripheral, but strain my eyes in the process. Like a deer in the woods, I hold my breath and avoid making any sudden movements in hopes of not drawing any attention to myself. Crossing my fingers, I pray he just walks on by because I'm not in the mood for whatever he has to say today. The sound of each foot fall gets louder on the marble floor as the sound carries across the reception area like a wave crashing into the shore. I am the shore.

"Good morning, Olivia." His strides stop directly in front of me on the other side of the shared, two-tiered reception desk. His rich baritone voice reverberates across the wood surface. "And of course, good morning to you Charlotte."

Damn it. I didn't want his shit today, let alone this early in the morning. Who did I piss off in another life and what do I need to sacrifice to make the world right again?

"Good morning, Mr. Pierce," Olivia purrs, her long legs cause her to bend at the waist while she stands and rests her elbows on the desktop, her chin perched on her hands. She bats her eyelashes for good measure. I can't fight my eye roll over her overzealous display.

Turning my attention back to the man in front of me, I plaster on the fakest smile I can muster. "Hi, Bennett. And for the millionth time, my name is not Charlotte. It's Charlie." I tap the gold nameplate sitting on my desk. "It's right there. Char-lie." I look up into his intense, aqua marine eyes. Big mistake. I get lost in his hypnotic gaze. He rests his forearm on the desktop, leaning in to get a little closer. Notes of citrus and a hint of leather swirl around me. Damn, he smells good. Heat flames over my cheeks, and for a moment all my thoughts disappear. Poof. Gone. One look at this gorgeous man and I lose my ability to think. Releasing myself from his trance, I pick at a piece of paper on my desktop as a lock of hair falls over my face. After a brief pause, I tuck the strand of hair behind my ear and focus my gaze on Bennett. "If my name was Charlotte, the nameplate would say Charlotte. Now, if you don't mind, I must get back to work." I swivel my chair around and shuffle some papers to distract myself and pray he gets the hint. I don't know why I let him get to me.

He releases a quiet chuckle before he turns, his footsteps growing distant on the marble floor. Then they stop. "Oh, by the way…" I startle, papers fluttering to the floor at the sound of his voice, and I lift my head in his direction. "I have a few clients arriving in about an hour. Two blondes, long legs, you can't miss them. Send them directly up to my office when they get here. We have *work* to do." He emphasizes work with a smirk on his smug face. "Thanks, Not Charlotte." He winks and turns on his heel.

"He's like an Adonis. How can you not appreciate a guy with an ass like that?" Olivia says, forgetting about using her inside voice. She's leaning so far back in her chair I'm waiting for her to topple over.

"I heard that." Bennett's voice carries through the open space as he continues his journey to the bank of elevators on the opposite side of the reception area.

Heat floods my face as I drop my head to the desk. Of course, he heard that. He doesn't need his ego stroked any harder. No doubt he gets it stroked daily, and I'm sure the two blondes will take turns stroking it too.

Olivia is still staring, and I snap my fingers in front of her face to break her Bennett induced haze. "How can you appreciate a guy who's an asshole like that? I've worked in this building with him for nine months. You would think he could get my name right? If he isn't calling me the wrong name, it's Ms. Hansley. In fact, I prefer he call me that. And what's with the comment about the two girls? And the wink? Ugh, he disgusts me. I like it when he just quietly sneaks in through the back entrance or better yet, when he doesn't come to the office at all." Venom laces my tone.

Olivia nibbles her lower lip. "I bet he would murder a girl's back entrance."

"Oh my God! What is wrong with you?" I think it might be time to put out an ad for a new best friend. Wanted: A best friend whose kind, loyal, and doesn't want anal sex with the biggest jerk in the office.

"What?" She shrugs. "It's been way too long since someone else has touched me. You know those 'days without sex' memes. I swear they were written about my life. Like day five hundred fifty-three without sex…I bought a box of popsicles just so I could have something in my mouth."

"Did you really?" I quirk an eyebrow questioningly.

"Not the point. Anyway, this isn't about me—" She places her pink manicured hand on her waist and juts out her hip. "You know, he says those things just to get under your skin. Every time he's in the office, he comes to the front desk to see *you*." Olivia pauses, her other finger tapping her pouty lips. "Now that I think about it, he probably has the hots for you. Guys don't know how to be adults and actually tell a girl they like them. They play those games of 'I'll be a jerk and maybe she will like me'."

"He's a jerk alright, and that's it. He's like thirty-three, thirty-four years old, not five. Mature adults don't act like that." I wave my hand to where Bennett once stood. "So, there is no way he likes me, and I don't even want him to like me." When I glance up at Olivia, her head is tilted while she studies me. Shaking my head, I swivel my chair around, ending the conversation. My once amazing Friday is slowly becoming a day from hell. Just then, my gaze catches sight of the white pastry box next to me with The Sweet Spot logo on top. Who says you can't have a cupcake for breakfast? Sometimes a girl just needs to eat her feelings.

A while back after a bad breakup, Parisa brought in cupcakes for Olivia in hopes of cheering her up and since then we've started a Friday cupcake tradition. We take turns buying cupcakes every week. Olivia switches it up between red velvet and lemon blueberry, while Parisa gets whatever her sister, Hollyn, has baked for the cupcake of the day, and I get vanilla. I flip open the lid and snag a fluffy cake. Just as I take a bite, Parisa storms through the glass doors, bags draped over her shoulders and hands full of poster board in various colors. Her medium length, wavy auburn locks cascade over her shoulders. With her brows furrowed, she drops the bags on the floor next to the desk. Even when she's frazzled, she still looks gorgeous.

"This day over yet?" She releases a huff, blowing a strand of silky hair out of her eyes.

"It's Friday. Why are you so stressed? Come out with us. Drinks after work," Olivia says.

"I wish I could, but I have this presentation to finish for Monday morning and it needs to be perfect. I overheard the marketing director is going to be retiring soon, so I will be doing everything in my power to get that position. But Seth has thrown a whole wrench in my plan as *he* now wants the position as well." She narrows her eyes and releases a loud exhale. "So, I will spend my day and probably my entire weekend perfecting this presentation so I can kick his ass." Parisa grabs a couple of the bags and hoists them up to her shoulder.

I nod and extend my hand holding the frosted baked good towards Parisa. The sweet, sugary scent wafting around the space. "Cupcake? They make everything better. And let me say your sister out did herself with these ones. Look at the flawless piping."

She eyes it closely. "Is that a vanilla cupcake with buttercream frosting?"

"Why yes, it is." I wiggle the cupcake in front of her.

"I'll pass for now, maybe after lunch when I'm in need of sugar. You always get vanilla with buttercream. Why don't you try switching it up everyone now and then?"

I shrug my shoulders. "I like vanilla. It's never let me down. There are no worries if I'll like it or not because I already know I do."

"You're so predictable. Live a little," Olivia says.

Flinching at her words, I cast my gaze downward pausing for a moment before reaching for the pastry box, flipping open the top toward Olivia and Parisa. "But I got some with candy pearls."

Parisa laughs as she collects the rest of her bags. "So dangerous. Watch out for that one." She nods in my direction. "But drinks next time because I will need it." She walks away but turns around, continuing her stride backward. "And if you see Seth come in, be sure to tell him I said to eat shit." With that, she swivels back around and hustles to the open elevator to go to her cubicle on the second floor.

I eye the cupcake still in my hand, shrug, and lick the frosting. What's wrong with liking what I like? Because this cake is so soft and fluffy, the smooth, light, airy buttercream frosting seducing my tastebuds with each lick. This is like an orgasm on steroids, maybe even better, because I know what I'm getting every. *Lick.* Single. *Lick.* Time.

CHAPTER TWO

Well, I fucked that up

Bennett

The soft click of the door sounds behind me as my feet carry me to the front of my desk. I press my hands to the varnished mahogany top as my shoulders slump. I draw in a long breath through my nostrils.

How does this girl keep affecting me this way? My head says to stay away, but my body wants more. So much more.

I round the desk and take a seat, linking my fingers behind my head as I lean back. Seeing her get flustered and her cheeks turn a rosy pink turns me on. She always gets shy around me, using her smooth chestnut locks like a curtain to hide behind. Closing my eyes, I picture her on her knees in front of me while I tuck the loose strands behind her ear, giving myself a full view of her beautiful, oval face. Her bright hazel eyes peer up at me while she sinks her teeth into her pouty bottom lip. My cock swells, straining uncomfortably against my zipper at the thought. I reach down and readjust myself in my slacks. Dammit. I don't need these two women thinking I'm hard because of them.

Since the first day I saw Charlie sitting behind the desk

almost a year ago, I was instantly enamored by her presence. Her warm smile would light up the darkest of rooms. But like the dumbass I am, when I saw her name plate, I assumed her full name was Charlotte. The sparkle in her eye diminished and was quickly replaced with something more along the lines of the repercussions of poking a bear with a stick. Something inside me really liked the way her cheeks flushed as she squared her shoulders, lifted her chin, and corrected me, so I continue to call her Charlotte. Knowing that she hates it also reassures me that there won't be a chance of any late-night rendezvous between us. I'm not in the market to find love. I'm here for the paycheck and as my bank account grows with each passing day, it encourages me to stay focused.

A loud knock pulls me from my thoughts and the door shoots open before I can answer. Trey and Seth stroll in, arguing about the baseball game last night. Seth seats himself in one of the leather armchairs in front of my desk as Trey takes the other.

"Just make yourself at home. I wasn't preparing for anything important," I mumble to myself as my eyes dart between the two.

"That's right. The two blondes who've been coming in and out of your office for the past month. I hope someone was coming with all those visits." Trey wiggles his eyebrows as he stretches back in the chair.

Seth straightens in his seat, adjusts his black frame glasses, and turns his attention to Trey. "Why is it always about sex with you? Why can't two women meet with Bennett because they want to purchase some property? Bennett is the best in the business, so it's obvious why they would come to him."

"Have you seen those two? We place bets on which one will have the first nip slip. If one of them bends over, her snatch is on full display." Trey sits up and rests his elbows on his knees. "Feel free to tell me I'm wrong, but that doesn't tell me those two women are business motivated. Maybe get on Bennett's dick motivated, but definitely not business."

My chin jerks in agreement because he's not wrong. They've made multiple advances toward me that I've shot down every single time. I don't know if they're looking to score a deal or if they are just lonely housewives looking for some fun, maybe both, but I'm only interested in the money. But I like to have a certain brunette who works downstairs think otherwise.

Seth propels himself from the chair. His eyes lock on Trey. "I can't with you two." Then his gaze shifts to me. "And good luck with your meeting."

A laugh breaks from Trey's chest as Seth shuts the door behind him. "I suspect that first part was meant for me."

Several minutes pass with Trey telling me all about his latest hook up when my intercom buzzes. The timing couldn't have been any better. Trey somehow always manages to fall into bed with the crazy chicks. I'm surprised none of them have tried to fake a pregnancy. Hell, I'm surprised he hasn't gotten one of them knocked up. Trey rises to his feet, and I do the same. Walking to the closed door, I twist the knob to see him out.

Before Trey's through the doorframe, he grips my shoulder. "Now, don't do anything I wouldn't do. No, wait, do exactly what I would do." A mischievous grin covers his face as he knocks on the wall. "These seem well insulated."

"Get the fuck out of here." I laugh and push him the rest of the way out the door. Before I turn back to my office, I catch sight of Charlie stepping out of the elevator. The sunrays shining through the glass exterior cast a glow around her. Without thought, my lips spread into a wide grin. As if she can sense me, her head shoots up and her eyes lock on mine. She cocks her head to the side and her brows furrow. I tone down my smile as she struts towards me, a pink flowy blouse tucked into a navy pencil skirt that hugs her hips. A loud cackle draws my attention from Charlie to the two blondes who trail close behind.

"Sarah and Stephanie are here to see you, Mr. Pierce," Charlie says in a sharp tone. Before I can respond, she whirls around. I hold the door open as the two blondes enter my office, but my eyes stay fixed on Charlie. Her hurried strides carry her to the elevator like the place is on fire and she's about to get burned. When she's out of sight, I turn back toward the open doorway and close the door behind me.

After, the paperwork is signed, I make a mental tally of how many extra zeros will be added to my bank account. I escort the ladies down to the reception area. As we step off the elevator, I guide Sarah, I think this one is Sarah, to take my left arm and the other to take my right as we walk toward the exit. I tell them some stupid joke, knowing their over-the-top laughter will draw attention. Pausing at the front desk right in front of Charlie, I let the two women walk out the building on their own.

Adjusting my tie, I turn to Charlie with a smirk on my face. "Well, that was double the work with those two. So much energy. They wanted to keep going and going but a man needs a break."

Olivia shakes her head, a half-smile covering her face, but when I catch sight of Charlie my pulse thunders in my throat. She crosses her arms over her chest drawing my gaze downward before it drifts up. Her narrowed eyes and flaring nostrils stare back at me. If I had to guess, she's probably killed me about ten different ways in her head.

Her eyebrows pinch together. "You're disgusting."

"Me? I just gave the ladies what they wanted and believe me, they wanted it… bad." I flash her a boyish smile.

"Oh my god, I can't stay here and listen to this." Charlie pushes off her desk, throwing her chair backward, and shoulders past me as her quick strides carry her down the hallway. My eyes fix to her methodical placement of one high-heeled shoe in front of the other. I bite back a grin when my gaze travels up to her toned calves and the way her fitted skirt hugs the curve of her ass.

"If you stare any harder, your eyes are going to fall out." Olivia's voice drags my attention away from Charlie as she positions herself next to me. "You don't need to be such a jerk to her. She's one of the good ones. I gotta go check on my girl." Olivia slides past me to follow the path Charlie just took.

I went too far this time. I cringe at my asshole-ishness. My focus is on the empty hallway Charlie just vacated.

Fuck.

Asshole One.

Bennett Zero.

CHAPTER THREE

Sexkitten69 meet BigDTF

Charlie

"The party has arrived!" Olivia shouts over the crowd and the deep bass thumping through the speakers as we walk through the front door of Porter's Ale House. She's always one for a grand entrance but this bar is like our home away from home, so it's expected.

Like every other Friday night, this place is wall to wall people. Fried food and a rich, hoppy aroma waft through the air. Luckily, we find an open table alongside the bar. We squeeze our way through the crowd when I spot the owner and friend, Jake. I stretch on my tippy toes and give him a quick wave. As soon as he sees me, he throws a head nod in my direction as I point to the empty table we'll be sitting at. I know he'll take good care of us tonight.

A neon brewery sign hangs on the weathered wood plank wall and casts a dim glow over our table. Porter's has a dive bar charm but with a splash of industrial feel with exposed ductwork and barn wood and sheet metal décor.

Olivia shrugs off her blazer and hangs it on the seat back while our waitress places menus on the table. Before the waitress can get a single word out, Olivia's rattling off our food and drink order, then she looks at her name tag. "And, Melissa, keep them coming and there will be a big tip for you. We need it." She points her thumb in my direction. "Or at least she does." Poor Melissa looks like a bobble head trying to get everything written in her notepad.

I flop down on the bar stool and drop my head to the table, lightly banging my head on the wood top. Thump. Thump. Thump. The rest of the day at work went fine, I didn't see Bennett again since after the incident with the two blondes, but the conversation played on repeat in the back of my mind. Like the best friend she is, Olivia could sense something was wrong because this is the same conversation we've had on numerous occasions. It's like a game show. What did Bennett do to piss off Charlie this week. I'll take *Breathed in Her Space for Five Hundred*.

"Hey, none of that." Olivia rests her hand on mine. "You have two full days where you don't have to see that jackass."

Sitting up in my chair, I catch Olivia off guard. I need to stop letting him dictate my emotions. "You're right. Enough about Bennett. Enough about work. I don't want to think about it anymore. A fishbowl margarita is calling my name. Along with a basket of greasy french fries. Then I can pretend this day never happened."

I don't know what got into me today. Bennett just pushed all the right buttons, all at the same time. Maybe he should play the lottery because he won the jackpot with how to get under my skin. This has been the same routine since my first day. I should be used to it by now but nope. He comes to talk to me but nothing intelligent falls past his lips. His beautiful, plump lips. The bottom one just slightly larger than the top. And then his smile. That smile could melt an ice cube in a freezer. And the dimple in his left cheek would evaporate the puddle. Ugh, what am I saying? I have a boyfriend. A kind, caring, loving boyfriend…

"Oh! I never showed you the pictures from the other weekend. Jared took me to a cute little cabin up north. I sipped my coffee on the deck as the sun rose over the lake."

I met Jared nine months ago here at Porter's. He came to our table with a round of drinks and the rest is history. I dig in my purse for my phone and open the photos app. I slide my phone, screen side up, to Olivia. She swipes her finger, scrolling through the photos. "I spent the weekend dropping hints that I have two weeks until I need to sign a new lease for my apartment." I hold up my crossed fingers. "Maybe he'll get the hint and ask if I want to move in with him."

Olivia's shoulders deflate as her eyes lift to mine. "Is that what you want?"

"It's the next step, right?"

"Whatever you decide, you know I'll be happy for you. But I still think you can do better than him." Olivia continues to swipe through the photos. She has never been Jared's biggest fan. They've butted heads on numerous occasions, especially after the one time she claimed he was getting handsy with a waitress. She called him a dirty douchebag. He called her a nosy bitch, and I've tried to keep them separated as much as possible since. But even so, she's always there for me when I need her.

Melissa returns and places our drinks on the tabletop but then her hand stops midair with the basket of fries. When we both look up, all the color drains from her face. Her eyes are locked on my phone screen.

Hesitancy laces her voice as she speaks to Olivia. "I don't mean to pry, but I couldn't help but notice the picture on your phone." We all look at the picture I took of Jared sitting on a fallen tree at the shoreline. "That guy is a dirty, disgusting asshole."

"Excuse me? That's my—" I start to say, but Olivia shoves her pointer finger in my face, essentially shushing me. What is happening right now? How does she know Jared?

"Go on," Olivia says. "How exactly do you know this guy?" With her finger still pointing at me, we both stare at Melissa intently waiting for her answer.

"Jared, right?" We both bob our heads, confirming that she knows his name. "I met him a week or so ago on this dating app, FLIRT. We chatted on and off for a few days." She shifts her weight from one foot to the other. "A couple nights ago, we finally met at a restaurant for dinner. He said he only had enough money to pay for his meal. Then out in the parking lot he told me he had to get up super early for work but could spare a few minutes if I wanted to go back to his car and suck him off."

My jaw hits the table as Olivia spits her drink out everywhere. What the fuck? I'm speechless. I look at Olivia, eyes wide, for confirmation. Did I hear her right? I can't believe this is happening. I think back to Wednesday night. Jared bailed on me last minute, saying he had an extensive project to finish for work.

"That lying, cheating, bastard," I mutter under my breath. Suddenly my mind replays all the times he said he was running late or had to stay late for work. Or those business trips he had to take. Were those actually for business? My hands tremble as I stare at my phone in disbelief. How is this happening? Olivia flips through more photos just to confirm that my boyfriend was indeed the same guy she met online.

"I am so sorry. I had no idea he had a girlfriend." Melissa clutches her hands to her chest. "I know it doesn't make up for anything, but next round is on me," she says, turning around and almost taking out another waitress as she makes her way back to the bar.

At this point, straight tequila might be the only thing that will tamp down the anger. Before I can say anything else, Olivia speaks, "I knew that guy was scum. I'm sorry Charlie. You don't deserve that. You are so much better than him. He was lucky to have you."

It's not like we were on the verge of getting married, but I hoped to one day. We had been together for nine months. That had to mean something. Or so I thought. I guess it makes sense why, when his lease was up, he decided to sign a new one verses moving in with me, stating that 'he liked his apartment.' But truth be told, he wanted his own apartment to hook up with other girls. I feel like an idiot. How did I not see this coming?

"I gotta see this for myself." I grab my phone from Olivia and look up this FLIRT app and hit download. "Dammit, I need to create an account before I can see anything."

Olivia snatches my phone back. "Oh, I got this." I chuckle and thank God I have a friend like her. We're also going to need more tequila. Stat.

Half empty glasses of margaritas and stacks of shot glasses cover our table. It looks like a two-person frat party took place.

"Charlie. Charlie. Charlieeeeee. This is going to be the best thing ever. Why don't we get drunk more often and come up with more amazing ideas?" Olivia slurs as she passes me my phone.

I close one eye and squint while I try to read the fake dating profile she created for me. "You picked SexKitten69 as my username? What the hell?" I squeak out. "I'm going to have all the creepers trying to creep on me."

"Good! That's the point." She shoves her finger at me before leaning across the table. "The biggest creeper of them all won't be able to resist a name like that. And then we will catch him red-handed in his jackass cheating ways."

I stare down at the profile picture she chose. It was taken a few summers ago when we were down by the lake. The sun is at my back, the light rays cast a halo around my bowed head. My hair drapes in front, covering half my face and my partial smile. Olivia turned the original color photo to black and white to add a dramatic effect, but it also makes the picture less distinguishable.

A few minutes was all it took to track down his profile. "He has the audacity to use a picture I took from our cabin weekend!" I screech. I never expected myself to be the person to plot someone's death but here we are, thinking of all the ways I could kill Jared and not get caught. "You know, I've heard if you plant an endangered species over the body—"

"What are we planting?"

Quickly dismissing the thought, I look up to Olivia, hesitancy lacing my voice as I say, "Nothing." I rest my elbows on the wood tabletop. "What's wrong with me? What makes me so unlovable?" A heaviness takes over my body. I hold up a finger. "First, there was Marcus. He wasn't ready to settle down but then five months after we broke up, I heard he was engaged. And now Jared."

"Charlie, there is nothing wrong with you. You just love too easily. And all these guys are dumbasses to let such an amazing girl like you slip through their fingers. What do they say, you have to kiss a lot of assholes before you find one you can tolerate?"

"That's not how that goes."

Olivia waves me off. "Either way, your guy is out there. He just hasn't found you yet."

A humorless laugh falls from my lips before I drop my head to the table, cheek resting on my forearms, my shoulders shuddering as a sob gets trapped in my throat. I always manage to find the jerks. Like the one time when I wanted to go the Van Gogh exhibit at the museum because it was the last day, but Jared wanted to watch the baseball game with his buddies. Guess who went to the museum by herself because *someone* couldn't spend one afternoon doing something I wanted. The fact I tolerated his behavior for as long as I did makes me feel even more sorry for myself. Pity party table for one, please. Actually, let me invite my friend Jose Cuervo. Just then Olivia waves a shot under my nose like smelling salts. When my eyes shoot to her face, she's wiggling her eyebrows at me, and I know she's not going to let me feel sorry for myself any longer.

Several hours pass, along with another round of margaritas, when my gaze homes in on a couple a few tables over. The guy is nuzzling her neck from behind as her head is thrown back in laughter. His hands wrap around her stomach, holding her tight as her fingers lace with his. Instead of having that tonight, I found out my boyfriend is a cheater and I'm drunk. Tequila drunk. Nothing good ever comes from a tequila drunk, and to prove my point, not only did we create a fake profile on FLIRT, but we found Jared's profile and started sending him messages, hoping he'd take the bait. We took a shot. Sent a message. Shot. Message. Shot. Message. But it's been crickets on the receiving end.

I pull up my Uber app and request a ride back to my place just as Olivia returns to the table from paying our tab. I make a sweeping motion over the table and slur, "It's time to go home and regret all this."

Want to know what death feels like? Drink copious amounts of tequila and wake up the next day. I'm never drinking again. I roll over and sling my arm over my eyes to hide the blinding sun that's pouring through the sheer curtain. I crack open one eye to check the time. Ten o'clock. It's still too early. I release a groan as I roll back over to sleep, but my bladder is telling me otherwise. Slowly, I slide out of bed as to not disturb my unsettled stomach. With careful strides I make my way out of my bedroom and to the bathroom, but first, I peer towards the couch but don't see Olivia. That girl was probably up and out the door as soon as the sun came up. She can drink like a fish the night before and run a marathon the following day, not that she would run a marathon.

After my quick bathroom stop, I walk into the open concept kitchen and living room. I live in a quaint two-bedroom apartment. Even though their idea of a second bedroom is more like an oversized closet, so I use it as such. While I like my designer labels, my wallet doesn't, so bargain hunting, consignment shops, and hand me downs from Olivia have become my go to, luckily, we happen to be the same size. Shocked was an understatement when Olivia gave me a pair of Louboutin heels because they were last season. I wasn't about to say no to that.

Ambling through the kitchen, I snag a water from the fridge and the bottle of ibuprofen from the cupboard. As I pass the picture window, I tug the curtain closed, and pull the Sherpa lined blanket off the back of the couch before flopping down onto the pillowy cushion. I'll just sit here and not move until everything stops spinning.

I spend my afternoon napping, scrolling through my social media, more napping, and getting lost in a sea of pins on Pinterest. I found some good ones on indoor gardening. Placing my phone down next to me, I reach for the TV remote when an unfamiliar notification tone chimes from my phone, making me pause. Curious, I grab it to and notice a small heart icon in the upper left-hand corner. Then recognition set in, and my eyes go wide as the phone falls from my grasp landing on the couch cushion. I scramble to pick it up, my fingers tremble as I dial Olivia. My heart beats in my throat as I listen to the ringing on the other end. *Pick up. Come on pick up.* I chant to myself. "He messaged back! What do I do?" I burst out, flailing my arm not holding the phone as I rise to my feet.

"Well, good afternoon, drunkie. Glad to hear you're alive," Olivia says chirpily.

"Jared messaged back on FLIRT. What do I say? This is uncharted territory here. He's going to know it's me…" I ramble incoherently.

"Calm down, he's not going to know it's you. Give me fifteen minutes. I'll be right over."

Olivia hangs up, and I pace around my apartment, unsure of what to do. This unease in my belly is either from nerves or the tequila wanting to make a reappearance. It's hard to tell at this point. Pulling up his message again, I read the words over and over. Wait, can he see I read it? Looking up I shift my gaze back and forth. Shit, too late now.

After what seems like the longest fifteen minutes ever my door intercom chimes letting me know Olivia's here. I race to the door faster than what I thought was possible in my hungover state to buzz her in. A few seconds later she's barreling through my door with two coffees and a pastry bag in hand. "I brought you my go-to hangover cure." She holds up the bag. "Let me see this message dickwad sent."

"Wait, how do you look like a supermodel right now?" I look down at my oversize bathrobe and fuzzy slippers. "I barely had the energy to get out of bed after last night."

"You know I can't just lay around all day." She wiggles her fingers at me. "Gimmie your phone." Once I drop my phone in her hand, she immediately scrolls through our messages from last night. I watch in part fascination and part horror as her expression change from humorous, to disgust, to anger. "What a piece of shit! We got this douche right where we want him." Olivia glares at the small screen. Peering over her shoulder this time, we re-read the messages, starting with the ones we sent last night.

SexKitten69: Hey big boy. It's a goood thing I have my library card because I'm totally checkin u out?

SexKitten69: Are u a parking ticket? cuz youve got FINE written all over u.

SexKitten69: Did u just come out of the oven? cuz ur hot.

SexKitten69: We should meet up? You can pet my kitten. Wink wink

"Did we type out wink? What the hell is wrong with us?" A laugh escapes me.

"Oh, just wait until you see the response." Olivia cringes.

Just then my phone rings and we both scream. Olivia does a juggling act with my phone and secures it before it crashes to the ground. Jared's name and number flash on the screen.

My heart thunders in my chest. "Why is he calling me? Do you think he knows?"

"Maybe he's calling to say hi because you're still his girlfriend."

"Shit. You're probably right."

Silence fills the room as the screen goes black. I release a sigh of relief, but it's short lived when the phone rings again. But this time I press the green talk button.

"Hello? Oh, sorry. I was in the uh… bathroom." I cringe at my inability to think of any other place like the bedroom or hell even on the other side of the room. "Today?" My eyes flit around the room as I try to think of an excuse. I fake a few coughs before saying, "I'm not feeling so well. I think I might be coming down with something." I pause. "Oh, no. You don't need to come here. I don't want you to get whatever I have. I'll call you later." I fake a few more coughs for good measure before pressing the end button.

Olivia barks out a laugh. "You won't be winning any Oscar's with that performance."

"Well, it seemed convincing enough for him. I want to see the rest of these messages."

I open the app and hold out my phone between us so we can continue reading.

BigDTF: Know what's on the menu?
Me-N-U

BigDTF: Let's make it happen.

CHAPTER FOUR

I'm not a creeper

Bennett

"Oh, come on," I grunt, pushing forward to gain more leverage. "Ah, that's it. You can do it. Almost there. Just a little bit more." Finally, I feel the release. I freeze for a moment as I exhale a sigh of relief and then sit back on my haunches. Wiping the sweat from my brow with the back of my hand, I gaze at the vision in front of me. "Out of all the times I've done this, I've never had one as stubborn as you." Loosening my grip on the wrench, it falls to the freshly cut grass. The late spring sun heats my back as I stare at the antique wooden wagon I've been working on for the past three weekends to give to my sister. Restoring and repurposing old farm equipment, along with various woodworking projects, has been a hobby of mine. Most of my clientele are family and friends, but the word seems to spread faster with each new project. I finish replacing the last bolt and tighten the nut into place. "This is a beauty," I whisper to myself. My sister, Liana, is going to love it. I fish my truck keys out of my pocket so I can load the wagon onto the trailer. Pulling out my phone, I block the afternoon sunlight as I check the time. Shit. I better get cleaned up before Sunday dinner. My mom and sister will give me hell if I arrive reeking of grease and perspiration and looking like a vagrant who just crawled out of the dumpster.

As soon as my tires hit the loose gravel in Liana's driveway, she's running down the front steps, a beaming grin plastered across her face. These are the moments I live for.

Growing up, we didn't have much, but we had what we needed. After my parents' divorce, Dad took off and Mom took on both parenting duties. Taking care of a six-year-old boy and seven-year-old girl was not a simple task, but Mom handled it like a champ. She always made sure there was food on the table, clothes on our back, and a roof over our heads. I can't say we had the latest new toys or designer clothes, but we didn't need that. We didn't care about that. We had each other, and that was enough. So, to see that smile on Liana's face always puts a grin on mine.

I open the door, and before I have both feet on the ground, Liana has me wrapped up in a tight hug.

"Oh, my god! Bennett, you're the best," she exclaims. After releasing me, she runs to the trailer to admire the wagon with a closer view.

Her husband, Mark, comes up to me, "You know she's going to have me moving that thing about twenty different times before she finds the perfect spot to place it."

"Yeah. I'll be sure to be busy that day." I laugh while slapping him on the shoulder.

When my sister finishes fawning over the wagon, we head inside. The smell of chicken parmesan permeates the room, making me salivate. With my nose leading the way, I climb the stairs from the split-level entry and pull out a stool at the kitchen island. My last home cooked meal was last Sunday when I was here for dinner. Otherwise, my meals consist of frozen pizzas, take out, or whatever restaurant a client wants to meet at. It's not that I don't like cooking, it's just that meetings, meetings, and more meetings occupy all my time and when I arrive home, I just want to kick back and relax.

"Here ya go, man," Mark says as he passes me a beer over the cascade white quartz countertop. I twist off the cap and draw a long pull.

The sound of two sets of feet come barreling down the hallway. Each kid takes a leg and squeezes. After the squeals of delight subside, I set my beer on the counter before kneeling so I'm at eye level with my niece and nephew. "Hey guys! Guess what? If you go into the back seat of my truck, I have a present for each of you." Their eyes go wide as their smiles before they ramble down the stairs and out the door.

"Bennett. You spoil them." When I stand, Liana is glaring at me, hand on her hip.

"I'm not going to win best uncle award if I don't, so…" I shrug before taking a long pull of my beer. Liana just sighs because she knows this is a battle she won't win.

"Fine. Fine. Keep spoiling my kids." She waves her hand in the air to brush away that thought before moving on to the next topic. "So, did you do it?" Liana's eyes sparkle as she flashes me a wide grin, her elbows propped up on the counter while she rests her chin on her hands.

I know exactly what she's going to ask. This is a rerun of the same conversation from last week's dinner and the week before that and the week before that.

"Yes, Liana. I did what you asked." For the past several months, my sister has been hounding me to get out and date. As soon as I graduated from college, my focus was on my career. I didn't want to get caught up in a relationship and settle down. Making a name for myself was my only goal. Sure, I dated here and there, but nothing serious. My longest relationship lasted sixteen months, and she kept hinting about a ring, getting married, and starting a family. Alarm bells sounded and I broke it off. Liana freaked out. Having another girl besides Mom at family functions is her lifelong dream. So, for the past eight weeks, and who's counting, all she talks about is me dating again. Numerous times she's offered to set me up with her single friends and friends of friends. Being set up on a blind date doesn't sound appealing. It's like someone else picking out your clothes. They may know what I like, but what if I don't want a suit and tie that day but jeans and a hoodie? And being thirty-four and trying to meet girls at the bar isn't as appealing as it once was. Trey's constantly hounding me to be his wingman, but I mostly do it to keep his ass out of jail. I swear the bar is the only place he knows how to find women.

So, to appease my sister, who thought it would be a fantastic idea, I set up a profile on a dating app. Supposedly, this is the new hip and trendy way to meet other singles and I will find true love because that's how her friend found her husband. Liana's words, not mine.

Digging my phone out of my pocket, I swipe to unlock it and pull up the FLIRT app and quickly flash her my profile page. "See, it's all right there. Giving this dating app the good ol' college try. Just for you, sis." I shoot her a devilish smile. I can't let her see the actual profile because then she'll know the picture I used isn't mine. Working with some high-profile clients, I can't have the city catching wind that I'm on a dating app. Many of them are already a little too flirtatious and touchy-feely as I show them properties. If they catch me on this app, they'll think I'm fair game. And let me say, some of those girls have no shame, like the one who not so discreetly took off her panties and set them on my desk before she left my office.

Liana squeals with delight. "You need to tell me everything! Have you made any connections yet?"

"Liana, give the guy a break. He just got here. Let him at least finish his beer before you drill him with questions."

I tap the top of my bottle with Mark's. "Thanks man."

"Why is it so wrong for me to want my brother to find love?" Liana looks up to Mark with big, admiring eyes and then leans into his side. He places a kiss on the top of her head. "It's not like he has any female friends who he could fall in love with, like us."

Mark and Liana are college sweethearts. It didn't take long for their friendship to turn into much more. Do I want what they have? To know someone always has my back. To have a girl waiting for me when I get home after a long day at the office. One who will listen when I need to vent when a business deal goes wrong. Until now, I've never thought about it. Grabbing my beer, I take a long pull, needing my mind to focus on anything else.

Just then my mom and stepdad, Dean, stroll into the house. I help my mom with the bags of food she brought over for dinner, and I give her a tight hug before shaking hands with Dean. Setting my now empty beer on the counter, I turn to Mark. "Hey Mark, why don't you show me that renovation project you're working on in the garage before the rest of the crowd arrives?" I need out of this kitchen, away from Liana and the thoughts she's putting in my head.

Walking through the door of my modern farmhouse. I drop my keys in the bowl next to the door, head to the kitchen, grab a beer, and throw myself on the couch. Twisting off the cap, I toss it onto the coffee table and kick my feet up. My family is exhausting with their game of twenty questions about Bennett's life. Not only did Liana get Mom on my case about my love life, or lack thereof, but she also recruited two of my aunts and a cousin. They're all now trying to set me up. Sometimes I wish my family didn't meddle in my business so much.

I grab my phone out of my pocket and my eyes land on the FLIRT app. I take a swig of my beer. I tap the app and red and pink hearts float up the screen while it loads. Why not look around? I'm scrolling, and scrolling, when a username catches my eye. What the hell kind of name is SexKitten69? I click on the profile and start reading. Everything else seems normal, but that name. A laugh rumbles from my chest. The green dot next to her profile says she's online. *Don't send her a message. Don't send her a message.* Too late.

Adonis21: Hey there SexKitten69. What does one have to do to make you purr?

Adonis21: That was creepy. I'm not a creeper. I promise.

The three dots next to her name bounce, but then stop. Shit, I totally creeped her out. I set the phone down next to me, but a few seconds later a ping catches my attention. Picking up the phone, I see her message.

SexKitten69: I'm not a creeper is exactly what a creeper would say.

Adonis21: Sorry. I promise, I'm a nice, normal guy. I saw your username, and it was just speaking to me. I had to message you. Haha.

SexKitten69: Ah, yes, this lovely name. You would actually be surprised at how many random creepers messaged me because of it. Or maybe you wouldn't, since you did the same thing.

Adonis21: Touché.

SexKitten69: I don't want to get your hopes up and think there will be some grand love connection here. I'm here because my boyfriend, well soon to be ex-boyfriend, is on this site. I won't bore you with the details, but this is more of a recon mission than a finding Mr. Right mission.

Adonis21: That's perfectly fine with me. I'm only here to get my sister off my case about dating. I've got nothing but time right now. So SexKitten69 how did the ex wrong you?

Hours later, I know the story about her piece of shit boyfriend and the waitress who found him on the dating app. While drunk, she and her friend derived this plan to set up a fake date so they could confront his sorry ass. I have to admit, this plan sounds fun. Definitely a shit way to find out, but it seems like she has a good friend in her corner to help her through everything. The clock on the wall adjacent to the television catches my attention when I notice it's close to one a.m. Work is going to come too soon. I type out a quick good night to SexKitten69 and stare up at the dimly lit ceiling. Rising to my feet, I click off the lamp and make my way to my bedroom. But I can't stop thinking about this girl. There's something about her that has me intrigued, besides being easy to talk to. It's refreshing to have a normal conversation with a member of the opposite sex. Maybe I could give this dating app a try.

CHAPTER FIVE

Well, that's a shame

Charlie

The early morning sun hits my face and I reach for my sunglasses to prevent the death rays from blinding me. I propel my legs down the sidewalk, weaving in and out of the people who are lollygagging like they don't have a care in the world, especially the one on her phone. *Move it lady, I need to get to work.*

A gust of wind assaults me from behind, causing my hair to whip me in the face, temporarily blocking my vision. I swat at the strands, but in my haste, I miss the orange caution cone informing walkers of the cracked cement. Lucky for me, the toe of my last season Louboutin pump, a gift from Olivia, finds the raised lip, hurtling my body forward as I take down a few unsuspecting victims before a concrete building stops me from face planting. My eyes cut to the path of destruction I just caused and my cheeks flame. Embarrassment roars through my body as the people on the ground shoot daggers in my direction. I offer a sheepish smile and mouth *I'm sorry* as I push off the concrete wall. If this is how my Monday is going to be, the rest of the week may kill me.

Before I reach the door of The Blue Stone Group, I glance around, making sure there are no other dangers lurking nearby. I deem the area secure and grip the long metal handle, but just as I pull, a guy in a suit is plowing his way out, paying no notice to who might be on the other side. *Asshole, watch where you're going.* My feet stumble backwards a few steps, but my grip on the handle prevents me from falling on my ass. Our eyes lock and I give him a curt smile, but secretly I want to choke him with his ugly, overpriced tie.

Gary, the building's middle-aged security guard, rushes through the doorway. "Ms. Hansley, are you alright?" His worried eyes roam over me to make sure I'm okay before holding the door open for me.

As I walk over the threshold, I offer him a small nod and thank him before giving him a half smile. I don't need to burden this man with all my troubles. I already did that to the stranger on FLIRT. Maybe I shouldn't feel bad? He asked as if he was genuinely interested. And it was a heavy weight lifted off my shoulders to unload everything from the past nine months. Sometimes you never really know how unsatisfying your life is until you view it from an outside perspective. All the signs were there. I just turned a blind eye to them.

Dropping my purse and bag on my desk, I take a seat and release a deep breath. I shouldn't feel sorry for myself. None of this was my fault, but it still just… hurts.

Olivia strolls in looking like she doesn't have a care in the world, and why would she? She's gorgeous, single, and no ex-boyfriend who ripped her heart out and left it on the ground for the crows to peck at. Ugh, I might need more time to wallow in self-pity.

"Good morning, sunshine. Are we ready to kick today's ass?"

"Nope. But you seem quite chipper this morning." I raise a questioning brow at her.

"A lady doesn't kiss and tell."

"And who said you were a lady?" I flash her a playful grin.

"Fair enough." Olivia leans her hip against the desk. "After I left your house, I stopped at the grocery store and ran into Trey in the ice cream topping aisle. A can of chopped nuts fell from my fingertips, and I watched his sculpted, denim covered ass bend over and retrieve it for me. All I could picture was him pouring chocolate syrup all over my body and slowly licking it off inch by delicious inch."

Reaching for a clipboard, I begin to fan Olivia before she spontaneously combusts. "What happened next?" I lean forward with anticipation.

"Oh, nothing." She shrugs. "I grabbed my chocolate syrup, smirked at him, and walked away. He's gotta work harder than that if he wants these goods." She dramatically waves down her body.

I can't help but snort out a laugh. If there is such a thing as death by blue balls, Olivia would be the Grim Reaper. She bolsters so much confidence, but truth be told, she keeps her heart locked up tighter than a Vegas casino bank vault. "Well, speaking of Trey, don't look now but he just walked in." I flash her a bright smile, but immediately see who walks in after him and disgust sours my mouth.

"Good morning, ladies. You both look radiant today," Trey says to both of us, but his eyes never leave Olivia. My gaze bounces back and forth between them, waiting for their eyes to turn into cartoon hearts and bulge out of their faces.

"Good morning, Char—"

Holding up my hand, I halt the rest of his sentence. "I'm not in the mood today, Bennett."

"She caught her sleezy boyfriend on a dating app, hooking up with a waitress from Porter's," Olivia says.

I shoot daggers in her direction, and she flashes me an innocent smile before making a hasty exit toward the break room taking Trey with her. I peek up at Bennett and he isn't laughing or cracking jokes. His eyebrows are drawn together, lips pursed.

"Everything okay, Charlie?"

Taken aback by him using my actual name, I just stare back, dumbfounded.

"I'm not trying to be a jerk or anything. That really sucks finding something like that out. I'm sorry," he says softly with his hand up like he surrenders.

I see the genuine concern in his eyes and sigh. He's not the bad guy here.

"Thanks. It caught me by surprise. It's over, but a part of me needs to see it for myself. Call me a glutton for punishment, I guess." Chuckling softly to myself. "Olivia came up with this crazy idea to create a fake profile and basically catfish him. We have a date set up on Wednesday at The Boat House. I get to catch this lying, cheating, bastard red-handed." What is with my word vomit lately? I think I've reached the point of not caring anymore. When I finish, I inhale a deep breath before glancing up at Bennett, the whites of his eyes are more prominent as his scruff covered jaw clenches.

"Uh. Well, look at the time. I got a meeting in a few minutes. Sorry to hear about the boyfriend. Hope you get the creep," Bennett sputters out before he swiftly turns and practically runs toward the bank of elevators.

Feeling slightly bewildered at his abrupt departure, I shake my head, dismissing his reaction. I don't have time or the mental capacity to dissect what a guy's thinking, least of all Bennett Pierce. Moving my mouse to wake up my computer, I busy myself with the copious amounts of paperwork and phone calls I need to finish before lunch.

While in the middle of composing an email a shadow casts across my desk and someone clears their throat drawing my attention away from the computer screen. Standing in front of me, a delivery guy shoves a white box in my face. I grab it before it tumbles to the desk. Inspecting the box, the familiar gold seal causes a smile to tug on my lips. When I look up, he's already out the door. *Well, that was kind of rude.* I flip open the top and inhale the sweet, sugary, vanilla scent.

"I know it's not Friday but due to the circumstances, I thought cupcakes were needed."

Lowering the box, I peer over the top as Olivia takes a seat. "Thank you. Cupcakes really do make things better." Reaching inside, I pull out two vanilla cupcakes piped with a vanilla buttercream. I pass one to Olivia and we tap our cakes together as if they were flutes of champagne.

At that exact moment, the clacking of heels echo through the atrium getting louder as they approach the reception desk from the elevator. A woman with sleek, midnight black locks comes into view. Her flawless skin creates an airbrushed look with her expertly applied makeup. The black knee-high skirt hugs her perfectly shaped body, but her boobs look as if they're about to spill from her button up white blouse. *Perhaps if she used a few more of those buttons we all wouldn't be graced with her exposed cleavage.*

"Can we help you?" Olivia asks using her fake overly nice voice.

"Oh no. I was just visiting Mr. Pierce." She tosses her midnight strands over her shoulder, which causes her to push out her chest.

Something about the way his name rolls off her tongue sends bile up my throat. Just another of the many women that parade in and out of his office. He must have met her at the other entrance because she never came in through the front. "Cupcake?" I shove my delicate cake in her direction.

Her face scrunches up with disgust as if I am trying to

feed her fish guts or something. "No thanks." She eyes me up and down. "I don't eat sugar. It does nothing for my figure."

"Well, that's a shame," I mutter under my breath. Opening wide, I take a giant bite of the cupcake. "This is so good. You're missing out," I mumble with a mouth full of cake. Sure, I have a little extra cushion in certain places like my stomach, thighs, and butt and I'm sure it's from the cupcakes, but they're my guilty pleasure. I won't let anyone take them away from me.

With that she turns and continues toward the exit. Olivia doubles over with laughter while I shove the other half into my mouth with a smirk on my face.

Several hours later, an inhuman growl sounds from my stomach, causing me to peer up from work to see if anyone else heard it. Apparently, cupcakes don't qualify as a hearty breakfast.

Parisa strides up to the desk lips pursed and ridged posture. "I need a break. Mostly, I need to get away from Seth and his particularly detailed nitpicking," Parisa says as she enunciates the last few words. "Food anyone?"

Olivia holds up her salad to-go container. "I got takeout, plus I have to go hunting for some missing paperwork. But there seems to be a demon child growling over there." She hikes her thumb in my direction.

"Yes, food. If I stare at this screen any longer, I might go cross-eyed." I toss my lightweight cardigan over my shoulders as we head out to a small bistro a few blocks away.

When we return to the office a big, beautiful bouquet of pink Asiatic lilies, Peruvian lilies, lavender daisy poms, and purple statices are perched on top of my desk.

"Olivia, these are gorgeous! You didn't have to do that." I rush up to the bouquet and inhale their floral fragrance. My fingers trace over their silky-smooth petals. One thing I need to do more for myself, get fresh cut flowers.

"I would love to take credit for those, but those aren't from me."

My gaze flies to Olivia and my brows furrow. Jared has never been one for flowers so why would he start now?

"They were delivered while I ran some papers to the second floor. Jan was down here so she must have signed for them." Olivia dives into the bouquet and pulls out a card. "What does it say?" Her wide grin on display as she holds out the business card size white envelope to me.

I slide my finger across the back, breaking the seal, and pull out a gold foil framed card. My eyes dance over the heavy, block capital letters.

HOPE THESE PUT A SMILE ON YOUR FACE.

-B

My gaze darts between the flowers and card still in my hand. Who would get me flowers? B? Who's B? These couldn't be from Bennett. Could they?

CHAPTER SIX

We have a dinner date tonight

Bennett

When Charlie mentioned she caught her boyfriend cheating via a dating app with a waitress from Porter's, my brain played connect the dots. SexKitten69 was Charlie, Charlie was SexKitten69. The same girl who I've spent countless hours messaging on FLIRT over the past four days. Most of it started off innocent, both of us just wanting to vent to a stranger about life but after a while the messages became exactly what the app is named for. Flirt. She's still clueless that I'm Adonis21 and I can't imagine she would be too happy with the idea, either. I'm sure, given the opportunity, she would push me off a cliff and spit on me on my way down.

Sitting behind my desk I rest my elbows on the desktop and scrub my hands down my face. What are the odds that this amazing girl I've been texting would be the same girl sitting at her desk on the floor below me? I click on the letter icon, opening my email, needing a distraction from my current thoughts. But instead of reading those emails, I'm pulling out my phone, reliving our text conversation from the other night.

Adonis21: How is my little Sex Kitten today?

SexKitten69: OMG! I need to change my name!

Adonis21: But I like how it rolls off my tongue. *Whispers* Seeeex Kitten

SexKitten69: Please never do that again!

Adonis21: Turns you on, doesn't it? *Wiggles eyebrows*

SexKitten69: Did we ever have that conversation about appropriateness? If not, we need to because all that is NOT APPROPRIATE!

Adonis21: I think you secretly like my inappropriateness. You picture me hovering over you, my lips almost touching yours. I'd have you purring like a sex kitten. I bet you're squeezing your legs together right now, trying to relieve some pent-up sexual frustration.

SexKitten69: I don't even know what you look like so how can I picture you doing anything.

Adonis21: Sends picture

SexKitten69: Is that two… four… six… pack abs. *drooling face emoji* But your head is cut off. I guess I'll just have to replace it with Charlie Hunnam. *shrugs emoji*

Adonis21: Did you just fuck swap me?

SexKitten69: Did I what???

Adonis21: Fuck swap… picture someone else's face while thinking of me.

SexKitten69: Huh… guess I did. *whispers* And it was worth it.

Adonis21: Gasp! No more pictures for you.

SexKitten69: Oh, how about one more for the spank bank. *winking face emoji*

Adonis21: Nope! I deserve one in return first.

I wonder what kind of picture she's going to send. Is it going to be something hot and sexy and stay true to the sex kitten name? Or is she shy and will keep it conservative. Several minutes pass and I haven't received a response, no bouncing dots like she's typing. Nothing. Shit, maybe I was too forward and scared her off.

Adonis21: Uh… still there?

SexKitten69: Sorry! I'm trying to get the right angles with the right lighting.

Adonis21: You're really putting a lot of thought and effort into this.

SexKitten69: Sends picture

Adonis21: *Picks jaw up off the floor*

SexKitten69: Well Adonis, me and the abs are going to go to bed now. Have a good night! *winking face emoji*

Adonis21: *Stares at picture* Uh, huh. You too.

I don't know how, but this girl makes the simplest picture seem so fucking hot. All I can see are her bare legs while she lays down on sheets that are rumpled around her. One leg is laying on top of the other, her right knee slightly bent with her feet partially wrapped in a blanket. The dim lighting casts the perfect glow to give the photo a seductress feel. What I would give to have those legs wrapped around my hips as I piston into her from above.

Closing the app, I toss my phone onto my desk, all my concentration is shot to shit. I now have a face to the name and it's the last person I would expect. Behind the screen she's bold, confident, and doesn't hesitate to challenge me, and that turns me on. Without a second thought, I reach for my phone and place a call to a local florist. Next, I dial Trey, telling him to meet me at the Blue Anchor. It may only be noon, but I need a drink. The Blue Anchor isn't our regular bar, but it's one place where no one asks questions. I gather up my things and get the hell out of here, purposely leaving out the back door to avoid any run ins with Charlie.

I'm finishing my second beer when the harsh sun lights up the dimly lit bar, catching everyone's attention. Trey strolls in and gives a head nod to a few of the locals who are scattered down the long, straight bar top. He spots me at the end of the bar almost immediately possibly because I'm the only one here wearing a two-thousand-dollar suit.

"It's a little early to be slamming them back, no?" He pulls out the stool next to me and sits.

Paper scraps litter the worn bar top as I pick at the label on my empty beer bottle before signaling the bartender for another. "You wouldn't believe me if I told you," I say over the low hum of the television in front of us playing highlights from last week's baseball game.

"Well, clearly this day is done, so lay it on me." Trey hails the bartender to get himself a beer as well.

"Guess I better start from the beginning. You know Charlie?"

"Yeah, she works the desk with Olivia."

I nod, confirming his answer. "She recently caught her boyfriend cheating on her through a dating app called FLIRT."

A deep v forms in his brow. "What does that have to do with anything?"

"So, I downloaded FLIRT to get Liana off my case. Later that night, I was bored and started scrolling to see what was out there and a profile caught my attention. SexKitten69. How could I not say something?" Trey makes a purring sound. "Exactly, I made a joke about making her purr and it got awkward for a moment but then she confessed she was only on the app to catfish her boyfriend."

"That's why I stay away from that shit. It just gets you in trouble." Trey takes a swig of his beer.

"Anyway, we spent the next few nights talking, then it turned to flirting, and some pictures were exchanged."

"Hell yeah. Show me the pictures." Trey eyes beam with delight as he reaches for my phone sitting on the bar top.

Before he can get to it, I grab it and tuck it into my pocket. "Fuck no. Because get this. SexKitten69 is Charlie"

"Wait, how do you know?

"SexKitten69 shared her story about the boyfriend with

me and then this morning Olivia spilled the same story about Charlie's boyfriend and the fake date tonight."

"Oh. Shit," Trey whispers.

"Yep."

"She hates you."

"Yep."

We simultaneously grab our beers, and each take a long pull.

"You going to tell her it's you?"

"That's the million-dollar question. I want to but I think she'll be less than thrilled it was me on the other side of the screen."

"Didn't you say she set up a fake date with her ex to catch him in the act? We need to go! I kinda want to see how this guy tries to weasel his way out of this." Trey throws his head back in laughter. "Plus, you can show up and be all knight in shining armor," he twirls his hand in the air like he's holding a sword, "and save her from the evil ex-boyfriend. Girls love that shit."

I want to laugh with him because the ex doesn't know what he's in for, but fuck. Charlie must be devastated by all this. I would be. To find out your boyfriend has been hooking up with who knows how many other women and for how long. She deserves better. Clasping Trey on the shoulder, he gives me a perplexed look.

"I hate to admit this, but you might be on to something. Thanks, man. Keep your phone close by. We have a dinner date tonight."

"How do you know what time this is going down."

I pull my wallet from my pocket and slam some bills down on the bar. "No worries. I'll figure it out."

"You always do." Trey holds up his beer to me while I turn and head out the door. I can't get shit-faced in the middle of the afternoon if I plan on making it to dinner.

Despite feeling good about the plan this afternoon, my heart rate spikes as I shift my Jaguar XJ into park several feet past the front entrance of The Boat House. Leaving the car running, I step out as the valet greets me to take the keys. This restaurant is swanky. Did the douche ex-boyfriend ever bring Charlie to a place like this? I round the rear of the car and Trey, my wingman for this operation, is already waiting for me on the sidewalk. Since he knows the ins and outs of everything that has happened, he's the perfect man for the job. Before we make it to the front entrance, rustling and whispers catch my attention. Then I hear her name. I wave to Trey to follow me around the corner and sure enough, I spot Charlie and Olivia roaming in the bushes next to a high arch window. Both Trey and I watch in fascination before I tell him to get our table and I'll meet him inside. Crossing my arms over my chest I can't hide the smile as I watch what's taking place in front of me.

"Oh my God, I can't do this Olivia," Charlie whispers.

"Yes, you can. Put your big girl panties on. You've been waiting all week to catch this fucker. Don't back down now." Olivia wiggles her way closer to the glass.

"No, I physically can't do this. These heels keep getting stuck between the rocks and I'm going to fall over. Not to mention, this bush has sexually assaulted me on more than one occasion."

With a broad smile on my face, I watch as Charlie crouches down, her tight dress perfectly molded to her round ass as she bats away the branch that she claims is currently assaulting her.

"I see that lying, cheating, asshole. Oh my God! He's even wearing the tie you bought him for his birthday," Olivia whisper yells.

Charlie maneuvers past Oliva to see for herself. "That is the tie I bought him."

"The nerve of him. I'm going to kill him." Olivia stands on her tippy toes to get a better view over the bush.

"You can revive him and kill him again after I strangle him with my tie," Charlie snarls.

"I like that plan. It will be like the *Groundhog Day* of his death."

Unable to help myself, I clear my throat and ask, "That's a little harsh, don't you think?"

CHAPTER SEVEN

I kissed Bennett and I liked it

Charlie

I stop dead in my tracks, my heart hammering in my throat. Where did that third voice come from? A deep, masculine baritone sound reverberates from behind me. I hate to admit but it's the same voice that has entered my dreams from time to time. Swatting the branch away, I slowly turn around, brushing off any loose foliage that may be stuck to my sequin jersey minidress as I carefully exit the rocks and step out onto the sidewalk. Olivia follows close behind.

"Oh, hi Bennett," Olivia greets. "You're just in time to watch me cut Jared's dick off and shove it down his throat."

I'm expecting Olivia to throw her fist in the air and let out a battle cry, but luckily, she stays collected, for now. My eyes linger on Bennett, dressed in black slacks and a white dress shirt with his long sleeves rolled up to his elbows. His forearms flex with each slight movement of his arms. The top two buttons at the neck are undone, leaving just a peek of what I'm sure is a rock-hard chest. My eyes drift upward. Based on the crinkle in the corner of his eyes and the cocky smirk plastered on his face, I know I've been caught admiring this fine specimen in front of me.

"That's right. The ex-boyfriend. And you're planning on doing this in the bushes?" Bennett raises a perfectly sculpted eyebrow. In two short strides his body is invading my personal space. He leans down to whisper next to my ear, his warm breath skating across my skin. "My advice is to not do that here. There are a lot of witnesses."

His low voice in my ear sends goosebumps up my arms as my nipples pebble against the fabric of my dress. *Tonight, was not a good night to go without a bra.* Finally, after what feels like minutes I pull back slightly, collect my thoughts, and nervously ask, "So, what brings you here?"

"Dinner with Trey while we go over work stuff for the big upcoming conference." He adjusts the sleeves of his shirt. "Speaking of Trey, he's waiting inside for me. You ladies have a good night."

Leaning in with his cheek almost touching mine, my eyes flutter shut as I breathe in his spice and leather scent. "Just know he's not worthy of you."

Slowly lifting my lids, his eyes lock with mine for a split second before he turns on his heel, his long legs propelling him down the short sidewalk until he passes through the double doors of the restaurant. His scent still lingers in the air. Instinctively, I inhale a deep breath through my nose to hold his fragrance with me just a little longer.

Olivia steps up next to me. "I could stare at that man walking away all day." I backhand her arm to break her out of her fantasy. She's just as boy crazy as a teenage girl. "Okay, okay… back to the task at hand. Let's take this jackass down." Olivia straightens her shoulders and puffs out her chest.

Suddenly, a wave of nausea runs over me. Confronting Jared in a room full of strangers, sure, but knowing Bennett and Trey are here… "I don't know if I can do this. There will be so many people watching. I should just wait until tomorrow."

"No! You need to catch him in the act, otherwise he's just going to come up with some bullshit excuse. If you do this now, he won't have an excuse." Olivia looks me in the eye. "You need to do this and then be done with him for good."

I inhale a deep breath, releasing it slowly. Olivia's pep talk sinks in. "You're right. I gotta do this now. So, let's do this."

My eyes take a few seconds to adjust to the soft lighting from the wrought iron wall sconces as we stride up to the hostess stand. This place is the epitome of romance with the rich, cherry paneling and the dark burgundy fabric draping down from the high ceiling. It's no surprise why Jared would bring his date here. He needs to pull out all the stops to charm her panties off, since his award-winning personality certainly can't do it. Just the idea that he would bring a random girl here spurs my hatred for him even more. But then my thoughts turn to Bennett. Why is he here? This restaurant is kind of out of place for him and Trey to talk business. Maybe they like the food?

Olivia guides me forward to greet the hostess. I inform her I'm meeting my party here.

"I'll be right here if you need anything, okay?" Olivia says.

I nod because I'm unsure what might spill out of my mouth as my head is filled with a tangled web of thoughts of killing Jared and Bennett watching. The hostess calls my name and directs me to follow her through the main dining room. High back booths line the perimeter of the room, small chandeliers fall over the tables, and the flicker of candles on all the tables creates a romantic ambiance. The sweet and succulent aroma of garlic butter mixed with a hint of sea salt fills the room, causing me to salivate. *Now is not the time to get hungry.* As we stroll through the dining room, I get the sense everyone is watching me, but really, they have no idea they came for dinner and a show. Without thinking, I scan the room to see if I can find Bennett and Trey, but instead I'm met with a wide-eyed Jared. After thanking the hostess, I swallow down my nerves as I pull out the chair across from him.

"Oh, look you got wine." Reaching across the table, I grab his glass, bring it to my lips, and swallow a big gulp. "Mmmm. This is good. Must be the expensive bottle." Reading the label on the bottle sitting in the ice bucket confirms my suspicion. I take a moment to assess his appearance. He's wearing the navy suit that I know has a hole in the armpit because he's too lazy to get it fixed. There's enough gel in his hair to host the slip and slide Olympics, if that were a thing. When our gazes meet, his eyebrows shoot up to his hairline, surprise written all over his face.

Jared leans over the table and whispers, "Charlie, what are you doing here?"

"You know, meeting my date. So, you must be BigDTF?" I say in a voice loud enough for others to hear.

It takes a moment for him to register what I just said. "Uh." His gaze shifts around the room before landing back on me. "I don't know what you're talking about, Charlie."

I point to myself. "SexKitten69. Sound familiar? You sent me a message wanting to meet up at this place." I gesture around the room. "After what, two days of chatting? You never took me to a place like this. Why is that? Saved that for all the other girls and not your girlfriend?"

Instantly, his face changes from shock to anger, the vein in his neck protruding. Jared pushes his chair back, almost hitting the table behind him, rises to his feet, and grits down at me. "You are creating a scene. This is not the time or place for these accusations."

Lifting myself from my chair I get in his face, not giving him the opportunity to talk down to me. "I think *you* are the one creating a scene," I challenge.

He grabs my wrist and attempts to pull me toward the exit. Yanking my hand back, I sneer. "You don't get to touch me anymore."

"Fine. But we are doing this outside." Jared turns and stomps toward the exit, and I follow close behind.

Standing along the side of the building, out of view of any onlookers, Jared gets in my face. "What the fuck, Charlie? To do that in front of all those people. What's wrong with you?"

"What's wrong with me? I didn't come to a restaurant expecting to have a date with someone who's not the person I'm dating." Venom laces my tone.

I dig my phone out of my clutch, open the dating app, and shove the screen in his face. "So, you're telling me this isn't you? It's the same picture you have splashed on all your social media accounts."

Jared tugs at his tie. "I mean, that's my picture, but someone must have stolen it. Shit like that happens all the time." His eyes soften. "Come on, Charlie, be smarter than that. Don't you trust me?" Jared takes a step closer, invading my space, and lifts my chin with this finger, forcing me to look up at him. The woody and spice scent from his cologne burns my nostrils as I suppress a gag.

Taking a step back to get some fresh air. "I don't."

From behind me, Olivia yanks my phone from my hand, her fingers flying across the screen. A phone notification sounds from Jared's jacket. He reaches into his pocket, checks the notification, and shoves it back in. Suddenly, a rapid fire of dings comes from his phone.

"Sure you don't want to get that?" Olivia smarts from behind me. Jared's lips press into a thin line as he reaches back into his pocket to retrieve his phone. Olivia holds out my phone to show a string of middle finger emojis sent through the FLIRT app. Jared stares at his notifications just as I peer over the top of his screen to see the same emojis.

"Jared, I can't do this anymore. We're done." My shoulders finally relax, and I stride past a shocked Jared. Twisting around with a hand on my hip, I had one more question. "Why'd you do it? Join the app?"

He stands there motionless, then lifts one shoulder. "I was bored. Everything became predictable." His tongue darts out to lick his lips, his voice low as he takes a step toward me. "Now, *this* Charlie. Where has she been for the past six months?"

I hold my hand up, halting his movement. Silence fills the space between us as his eyes bore into mine. I'm not sure what he's expecting me to say, but he's not worth any more of my time. Adrenaline surges through my body and for once, I'm taking charge. Spinning around I raise my middle finger to him as I walk away. I hope I never see his despicable face again.

Everyone was right. I deserve better. I can't believe I wasted nine months of my life with that ass. Staring at the pavement while I weave in and out between parked cars, the last ten minutes are on repeat inside my head. Until I suddenly hit a brick wall. My hands fly up to feel a strong, muscular man chest. *Okay, not an actual wall.* My gaze lingers on my fingers as they have a mind of their own and start slowly tracing the pearly buttons of a white dress shirt. The scent of citrus and leather fill my senses. Lifting my head up and up until I'm met with piercing blue eye staring back at me and then it hits me… Bennett. My hands fly off his chest as if I touched a hot stove.

"Hey, Charlie. You okay? I saw what happened back there. Well, the whole restaurant saw what happened." Bennett hikes a thumb behind him.

"You saw that? I'm so embarrassed." My hands fly to cover my face as heat creeps up my cheeks. I was hoping his table was on the other side of the restaurant. Now is the perfect time to find a hole to crawl into and die.

He bends at the knees, grips my wrists, and pulls my hands away so his eyes are level with mine. And I don't stop him. "Don't be. He's the one who made an ass out of himself. I guarantee you no girl in there is going to touch that asshole." Bennett stands to his full height. "What are you doing now? Want to get out of here? Trey and I were just about to head to Porter's for some drinks. You and Olivia should join us."

I feel slightly taken back by his offer because we were never the going out for drinks kind of co-workers. Perhaps that's because I spent most of the time hating his guts. Well, mostly, that hasn't changed. He's still cocky, arrogant, and a playboy. Perhaps I'm just not used to Bennett acting this way. But at this point, I have nothing to lose. I look behind me to see Olivia chatting with Trey and turn back towards Bennett.

"Yeah, sure. After the way this night has gone, I could use a drink or two."

"Okay, it's settled then. We'll meet you there in a few. "

Empty glasses and beer bottles are scattered across the tabletop. Olivia occupies the chair next to me while Bennett and Trey are seated across from us. We must be three or four rounds in, but who's counting. We've spent the evening sharing dating, hook-up, and one-night stand horror stories. My stomach feels like I did a thousand crunches from laughing so hard.

"You remember that one time while on spring break in Cancun. That girl took off her panties right on the dance floor and shoved them into your pocket." Trey smacks the table in a fit of laughter.

"Please don't remind me. That chick was a clinger. Would not leave me alone. There is desperate and then there is *desperate,*" Bennett says.

"What did you do?" I ask.

"We were dancing close to this other couple, and I kept creeping closer and closer to them. Eventually, I slightly nudged her toward them and took off."

"Dude, that wasn't a slight nudge. That was like a heavy thrust. I don't think I've ever seen you move so fast in your life," Trey says, pointing his beer bottle in Bennett's direction.

"Man, I drank so much but I was still coherent enough to know to not get involved with that one." Bennett raises his beer to clink with Trey's as laughter fills our table.

"I'm going to get us another round." Trey stands up and Olivia joins him as they collect the empties to bring them up to the bar. As I glance around, I notice the bar is considerably emptier than when we first arrived. What time is it? I check the clock on my phone and see it's nearing midnight. Damn.

"Hey, guys! I'm going to pass on that drink. Home is calling my name." Standing up, my legs feel like Jell-O, and I steady myself with the back of the chair.

"You alright?" Instantly, Bennett's at my side. He firmly grips my waist as his deep gaze lingers on mine.

A giggle escapes my lips, breaking his stare. "I probably should have stopped two margaritas earlier. Work is going to be fuuuuun tomorrow."

"Here, let's get you an Uber, Emberella. Don't want you turning into a pumpkin before midnight." Bennett pushes in our chairs before trailing behind me toward the exit.

"Shouldn't that be Cinderella?" I ask over my shoulder. Before he answers, we wave to Olivia and Trey at the bar. Bennett holds the door open as we step out into the cool, summer night air. Without even realizing it, I link my arm through Bennett's. To keep my balance? To feel his warmth on my body? Either way, I snuggle in closer, his masculine scent invading my senses. My fingertips graze down his arm and over the top of his hand. A jolt of excitement courses through my body from the touch. I don't know if it's because of this man, because I haven't felt genuine excitement in a long time, or because of the margaritas, but I don't want to lose this.

There's a moment of silence between us before Bennett speaks. "To answer your question, it's ember instead of cinder because like an ember you have a bright, beautiful glow surrounding you."

A smile tugs at my lips from his compliment.

"Opposed to a cold, black, piece of coal," Bennett finishes.

I playfully smack his chest and he flinches. His hand rubs the offending spot like he's wounded. "You did good until that last part. I'll just pretend you didn't say it."

Bennett spits out a laugh. "What's your address?"

I rattle off my address while he uses one hand to type it into his phone.

"That's not too far from here. If it wasn't so late, I would just offer to walk you home. But your curfew and all."

"Shut up, it's not a curfew. I just like my sleep. And I'm going to need all I can get if I'm going to be a functioning human tomorrow."

"Looks like your chariot will be here in ten minutes." He tucks his phone back into his pocket.

"Did you just order me an Uber? You didn't have to do that." Releasing my arm from his, I fish around in my wallet to look for some cash.

"Don't worry about it. It's on me." He offers me a sliver of a smile.

A piece of hair blows across my face, and I wrap my arms around myself to keep warm. I stare off into the empty street in front of me, waiting for the headlights of my ride.

Pulling me so I'm facing his chest, Bennett runs his hands up and down my arms, sending an electric current through my nerves. I lift my chin and his sharp blue eyes look down at me. "So, why the sudden nice guy act? I'll have to admit I'm not used to this."

Bennett looks up to the streetlight lit sky before releasing a soft chuckle. Then he brings his gaze back down to me. "Oh, that's right, girls only want the bad boys who break their hearts."

I rest my forehead on his chest, all the while his hands continue to rub up and down my arms. "Story of my life." I gaze up and our eyes meet. "Maybe that's my problem. I just need to find a nice guy."

"I'll have you know, I'm actually a very nice guy, or at least that's what my mom and sister would say." He winks.

"Oh, well if your mom and sister say that, then it must be true."

"Truth be told. You dealt with enough this week. You didn't need me giving you a hard time but next week might be a different story."

I bark out a laugh. "Well, that's good. I don't know what to do with this version of you."

We stare at each other for a few passing seconds. Unsure if it's because I'm feeling vulnerable and he's being nice or because I have tequila running through my veins, but I stretch up on my tiptoes, and place a soft kiss on Bennett's full lips. He doesn't move. Not his lips, not his eyes, not his hands gripping my arms. Pulling away, I lean back slightly to get a better view of him.

"I'm sor—"

Before I can finish, his lips crash against mine in a fury of heat and passion. His hand snakes around to my back, leaving a wake of heat as it travels upward into my hair. Gently, he tugs my strands, causing my head to tilt up to give him better access. His tongue coaxes my lips apart and I eagerly let him in. Our tongues caress each other in a seductive dance. A small gasp escapes from me as he pushes my back up against the rough cement wall. Bennett's hard body presses against mine. The bulge in his slacks pressing in my stomach as I rock against him. Needing more friction, I hike my leg up over his hip as he steps between my legs and firmly grips the back of my knee. All the noise from the bar and from the street seem to disappear into the night air. The only thing I can hear are my breathy moans and Bennett's heavy breathing. His hand skates up my bare thigh, causing goosebumps to prickle over my skin.

"Hey, are you the one who called an Uber?"

A voice pulls us from our lust daze. Bennett turns his head as I do the same. "That would be me." I raise my hand. Maybe I should just shoo him away so we can continue this grope fest.

Dropping my leg back to the ground, I stand to my full height. "Thanks for everything, Bennett. I really appreciate all that you did tonight." My lips twitch into a smile when our eyes meet.

"Don't worry about it. Have a good night."

"You too."

I walk to the Uber and open the door. Before getting in, I look back at Bennett and bite back a schoolgirl grin. He raises his hand in a small wave and I do the same. After I shut the door behind me, I press my fingertips to my lips. I just kissed Bennett Pierce. What was I thinking? And why do I want it to happen again?

CHAPTER EIGHT

If it was easy, it wouldn't be worth it

Bennett

As soon as the Uber pulls away from the curb, I watch as the taillights disappear into the night. Without thinking, I take out my phone and send her a message.

> **Adonis21:** Just wanted to say hi. I was thinking about you. Have a good night.

As soon as I press send, I regret it immediately. Will she know it's me? Or will she think it's a big coincidence? I never expected her to kiss me. I'm not complaining, but once she started, I didn't want it to end. I may have taken it too far by pushing her up against the wall, but her needy moans told me otherwise. I would like to blame it on the alcohol, but I've been attracted to this girl since the first time I saw her. My own goals forced me to keep my distance. Then she got the boyfriend, so she became off limits. I wasn't about to insert myself into someone else's territory, especially when I didn't have a reason to believe she was unhappy. Besides, mixing business with pleasure seemed like a bad idea. That's a surefire way for shit to blow up, costing both of us our jobs.

"Hey man," Trey says as he and Olivia exit the bar. "I'm going to give Olivia a ride home. You want one?"

"Nah, I'll just call an Uber. I'm on the other side of town, anyway."

"You sure? We don't mind," Olivia asks.

The pleading look on his face and flailing arm gestures tell me otherwise. "Yeah, you guys go ahead."

We say our goodbyes and they take off down the sidewalk and I leave in the opposite direction.

Once home, I shed my clothes and crawl into bed. With one last glance at my phone, I notice Charlie has seen my message I sent from FLIRT but hasn't responded. Fuck. What if she knows? She shared some rather intimate details she wouldn't have shared if she knew I was Bennett and not Adonis21 on the other side of the screen. It's funny how we'll divulge our deepest, darkest secrets to a stranger, confide in them, perhaps looking for an unbiased opinion or trusting that information will never be revealed. All her secrets are safe with me. The rest of the night is spent in a restless sleep, tossing and turning, and thinking about Charlie.

The next two days are spent working from home and setting up meetings outside the office. As much as I would love the distraction of Charlie, I can't afford to be distracted right now. I've been working with a client on the purchase of a five-hundred-acre commercial lot. If I can nail down this sale, it will catapult my career higher than I've ever thought possible.

My leg bounces as I wait at the table of Le Uve Bistro. Only a few people are scattered amongst the dozen tables.

While the restaurant is quaint, the views of Lake Superior are breathtaking, and the food is Michelin Star quality. "Good afternoon, Mr. Reid." I wipe my palms on my slacks before I stand and extend my hand to him.

"Good afternoon, Bennett. But call me John. We don't need the formalities." His firm grip clasps mine, his gold Rolex glinting in the sunlight. A bead of sweat forms on my brow. I hope I don't fuck this up.

"Well, John, I'm glad we could meet today. This is the perfect property for you." My foot hits the table leg, causing the clear water goblet to splash on the white linen tablecloth and the cutlery to rattle. "Let me get the papers…" As I reach down, my fingers fumble to grip the folder to pull out of my briefcase.

"All this business talk can wait a minute. Let's have a drink first. You seem a little nervous." Not waiting for my answer, John casually raises a finger to draw the server's attention.

"Get me an old fashion. Two Luxardo maraschino cherries," John says.

Without even thinking, I say, "I'll have the same."

"Okay, so Bennett, how are you doing? How's the family?"

John has known my stepdad for most of his life. His dad and Dean's dad grew up together. And I've known John since I was a high schooler working with Dean at his real estate agency. John has found his fortune by being very strategic with his investments. Most of them involve real estate, so when he called my office looking for a particular piece of land, I knew this would be huge. Family friend or not, I must treat this like any other business meeting. Be professional. Get the deal. And we both leave here happy.

"So, about these papers…"

"Cut the bullshit, Bennett. I'm going to sign the paperwork. No need to be nervous about that. But something tells me that's not it. What has you so distracted? Gut feeling says it's about a girl."

My brows knit together. "Why do you say that?" Reaching for my drink, I take a much bigger gulp than I should.

"I've seen that look. Hell, I've had that same look in my eye before. The longing. Like you want her but can't have her."

"Yeah, it's something like that."

"If all my years on this earth has taught me anything, it's don't hesitate. I did once and then I lost her. To this day I've always wondered what if?"

Easier said than done.

"It's complicated." I roll the bottom rim of my glass in circles on the table.

"If it was easy, it wouldn't be worth it." John cocks his head toward me.

Swallowing another drink, I let his words sink in. At first, I forced myself to not want her. Then I couldn't have her. Now's my opportunity, but do I risk it?

We spend the next hour talking business and his plans for the property. By the end of lunch, I tuck the signed papers back into my briefcase. I just landed the biggest deal in my career. I should be ecstatic, but the situation with Charlie sits at the forefront of my mind.

"Cheers, you lucky son of a bitch! I can't believe you got him to sign the deal." Trey hollers as he holds his pint glass in the air. I clink my glass to his along with Seth's. We all tap the bottom of our pints to the table before taking a swig. The guys wanted to go out for drinks to celebrate my big sale and there's no better place than Porter's.

"So now that you have all this money, where we going?

Guys trip. Hook up with some hotties in bikinis." Trey smirks.

Seth turns to Trey. "Sometimes I wonder if you have kids scattered across North America."

"No one has come knocking on my door looking to collect child support, so I must believe the rubber sperm collectors have kept me safe. But enough about me." Trey wraps his arm around my shoulder. "This guy here has the hots for Charlie down at reception."

Embarrassment creeps up my face. I've already spent all day thinking about her, so I wish my evening would be different. But guess not.

"Whoa. Where did this come from?" Seth asks.

Before I can say anything, Trey is spilling my entire backstory regarding Charlie to Seth. "The best part is he's been secretly stalking her on a dating app," Trey says.

"It wasn't intentional. I started chatting with a random girl on FLIRT and it just so happened to be Charlie." I shrug one shoulder, acting coy about the whole situation.

Seth turns to me. "So, you're telling me you've been talking to her online and she has no idea it's you?"

All I can do is nod. Laughter erupts around the table at my expense.

"If Charlie is anything like Olivia or Parisa, she's going to rip your balls off and stuff them in your pocket," Seth says through a laugh.

"Or down his throat." Trey counters.

"Nah, Charlie has too much class for that. She'd keep it reasonable. Olivia on the other hand, cross her and she'll put your balls in a blender."

We all cringe at Seth's remark.

"What about you, Seth? Any lady woes to share?" I ask.

Trey interrupts with a laugh. "Oh, you haven't heard. He's saving himself for marriage."

"Just because I don't make a spectacle out of every sexual

encounter doesn't mean it doesn't happen. I don't need to plaster billboards around town informing the community of who I'm sleeping with." Seth squares his shoulders while he adjusts his bow tie.

"I've never put up a Billboard." Trey quirks an eyebrow. "But that might not be a bad idea. It would be effortless. A fourteen-foot-high picture of me would certainly draw the ladies. Include my phone number. Boom. My phone would be blowing up."

"Your ego is fourteen feet high. Let's tone it down a notch. Plus no one needs to see your ugly mug on a billboard," I say, bursting Trey's bubble.

"It'd scare little children," Seth adds.

"Just imagine if they place the billboard outside a nursing home. All the old, single ladies would be dialing the phone," I reply.

Seth says with a laugh. "They need love too."

Trey points between Seth and me. "You guys are assholes."

"Also, I'm looking for a quality woman. Not just anything that walks and breathes," Seth says.

"I have to say, I find breathing a great quality," Trey counters.

Seth leans back in his chair. "Glad we don't need to add necrophilia to your resume."

Trey gives Seth a playful shove. "Now, if you'll excuse me. There's a blonde at the bar giving me fuck me eyes and I can't disappoint." Trey pushes his chair back and strolls through the crowd towards the bar.

"So, Charlie?" Seth breaks the silence.

I take a pull of my beer. "Yeah. I won't lie. It was a pleasant surprise when I found her on the app. What are the chances?"

"Just remember. She doesn't know it's you and if not handled properly this will all blow up in your face."

"Yeah. I know. I think about that every day."

Later that night, I'm lying on top of the sheets staring up at the pitch-black ceiling, the summer heat making me restless. Thoughts of Charlie race through my mind. My phone on the nightstand goes off, illuminating the dark space. Blindly reaching over, I snag it and see it's a notification on FLIRT.

Emberella55: Hey stranger.

My brows furrow, unsure who this is at first. Then it hits me. Shit, and she's used the nickname I gave her other night. Good to know she's thinking about me.

Adonis21: Oh, I see you went with a name change. Didn't want to be a sex kitten anymore.

Emberella55: Haha, I was one dick pic away from a BINGO. Big ones, small ones, hairy ones, ones that unnaturally curved to the right. Nothing is worse than an unsolicited dick pic.

Adonis21: As much as I want to talk about other guys dicks with you, I would rather not.

Adonis21: Just for the record, it would be the gentlemanly thing for me to say I wouldn't want any tit pics, but I'm not a gentleman. So, I'll welcome those. My inbox is always open if you get bored one night or something…

Emberella55: Ha! You're the worst! Also sorry for not

getting back to you the other night. Things kinda got weird for me. I kissed my co-worker. Then I've been in my own head since I haven't seen him all week. He probably regrets what happened and is ignoring me.

I re-read the 'I kissed my co-worker' over and over again. A little more invested in this conversation, I sit up and lean against the headboard. My heart feels like it's going to burst out of my chest. I wonder if she'll tell me more. Fuck. I feel like an asshole, but I need to know more. My fingers have a mind of their own as I type out the next message.

Adonis21: Hey. No problem. I've been there. Wanna talk about it? I'll be the unbiased third party.

Emberella55: Yeah, I don't know what to say. Hell, I don't even know what to think yet. He's a good-looking guy and he knows it. But he constantly has women going in and out of his office and he rubs it in my face with his snide comments. All the women could be part of his job, but I don't know… I'm just going to chalk it up to too many margaritas and feeling vulnerable.

Adonis21: Or you could talk to him…

Emberella55: That seems like a terrible idea. Hahaha, I don't even know what I would say to him. 'Oh, so we kissed, and I kinda liked it. We should do it again.'

Adonis21: You could say exactly that.

Emberella55: I just got out of a semi-serious relationship. What I really should do is just focus on myself. Do all the things I want to do. I could take up knitting. Would you like a Christmas scarf? I'll knit you one!

Adonis21: Uh… no offense, but no.

Emberella55: Oh, everyone is doing aerial yoga. It's all the rage. I could twist myself up in some fabric strung from the ceiling. You could join me!

Adonis21: I would rather take the scarf.

Emberella55: You're no fun!

Emberella55: But anyway, I just wanted to say hi. Early morning tomorrow. Thanks for the chat as always!

Adonis21: You should reconsider talking to this guy. He might be more receptive than you think.

Emberella55: Right! Good night!

Adonis21: Night.

So, she's been thinking about me. That must be a good sign. I know I sure as hell have been thinking about her. She's consumed my every thought since that kiss. A smile graces my lips as I close my eyes.

CHAPTER NINE

I don't need a man

Charlie

"I need you guys! STAT!" I sit crossed legged in the middle of my living room with my phone on speaker. Random balls of yarn, paint, craft wood, and glue lay scattered in a circle around me.

"I'm just pulling up to your building," Olivia announces through the speaker.

"I'm right behind Olivia," Parisa says.

Sure enough, a few minutes later they're buzzing my intercom to be let up, before I know it, they are walking into my apartment.

"What the hell happened here?" Olivia sets her purse on my kitchen island as her eyes roam the mess I've created.

"Looks like someone is doing some DIY therapy." Parisa stands next to Olivia.

"I couldn't sleep. Then I wanted a distraction. And then I ended up with this." I hold up a scraggly looking scarf. "And this." I search around until I find the leaf mason jar candle holders, I tried to make but wound up with strings of hot glue resembling a spider web. "I think something is wrong with my glue." I hold up the hot glue gun.

Olivia holds her hands up. "Whoa, put the glue gun down and step away from the innocent crafts."

"Wait, I haven't seen her this frazzled with her crafts since the first time she kissed Jared. Oh shit, please tell me you didn't kiss Jared." Parisa's wide eyes stare at me, waiting for an answer.

"Hell no. I'm done with him." I drop my head to my shoulder, avoiding eye contact with them as I mumble into my shirt. "But I kissed Bennett."

"What was that?" Olivia asks.

Heat creeps up my cheeks as I gaze at my two best friends. "I kissed Bennett." As soon as the words are out of my mouth, I cover my face with my hands. Now that the words are out there, I can't take them back.

"Damn. I wasn't expecting that." Parisa flops down on the couch in front of me.

"I was with you last night. When did this happen?" Olivia takes a seat next to Parisa.

I rehash the events that took place last night all the way up to when the Uber took me home. "I don't know what to do?" I fiddle with some ribbon laying in front of me, needing anything to distract me from what I know will come next.

"Did you enjoy it?" Parisa leans in, waiting for the scandalous details.

My teeth sink into my bottom lip as I think about his lips on mine, firm yet sensual. The way his fingers dug into my thigh as I wrapped my leg around his waist. Feeling his bulge pressed against me, knowing I did that to him sends a jolt of electricity through my body all over again. "Let's just say, I don't remember the last time I've been kissed like that." Then the high I was riding dies a slow, painful death. "But it's Bennett and who knows how many girls he's kissed with those lips." We sit in silence for a few moments. "Who am I kidding, I'd been drinking, he'd been drinking. He was probably just looking for a warm body."

"Didn't you kiss him first?" Parisa asks.

"Call it a lapse in judgment. I'm solely blaming it on the tequila. He caught me at a vulnerable moment, and it just happened."

"See, I knew he liked you." Olivia shrugs her shoulders.

"But we work together. Hypothetically, say we start dating and then it didn't work out. We would still have to see each other every day. I don't need that kind of stress in my life."

"Stress? Are you kidding me? Hot office sex is where it's at." Olivia wistfully gazes into the distance. I'm sure imagining what hot office sex would be like.

Sitting up a little taller, my gaze dances between Olivia and Parisa. "On second thought, I'm going to focus on me. No more guys. No more dating. Just me."

"Charlie, you know I love you, right? So don't take offense to what I'm about to tell you, but you are a serial monogamist. You can't be without a guy. You've always had a boyfriend," Olivia says.

Taken aback by her comment, my jaw drops. "Lies! I am not a serial monogamist."

"Oh yes, you are. You like the comfort of a guy on your arm." Olivia holds up her fist, releasing a finger with each name she recites. "We will work backward from Jared. Then before him was Marcus. Then semi relationship, fling with… what was his name…"

Rolling my eyes. I deadpan, "Chris."

"Ah yes Chris. How could I forget Chris? Now, why didn't it last with him?" Olivia pretends to think when she knows exactly his problem, but she just wants me to say it.

An exasperated sigh escapes my mouth. "He kept his socks on during sex."

"Ah yes. Socks were a deal breaker."

All three of us giggle. "Some things are a hard pass. And

Marcus wasn't my fault for the record. But I'm going to prove you wrong. Today marks the day that Charlie Hansley takes a break from dating."

Olivia jumps up from the couch and runs into the kitchen opening and closing drawers.

"What are you doing?" I ask.

"Looking for a pen and paper. I need to get this in writing."

Finding a pen next to me, I throw it at her. "Oh, shut up. I can do this. I don't need a man."

"No one needs a man," Olivia exclaims. "We just want one. Especially for those extra lonely nights. Speaking of which, it might be time to pay a visit to the toy store. You might need something new to get through those lonely nights."

Jared was very vanilla when it came to sex. Never wanting to be too adventurous. Sure, he would get me off, most of the time, but it soon became routine, and I became complacent. Maybe the idea of toys demasculinized him, or he just saved that for all his mistresses.

"I'm in."

Olivia perks up. "Let's go."

CHAPTER TEN

I can step outside my box

Charlie

To any passerby, the enormous, steel, windowless building would look like a place where people go to get murdered, but to us it's The Pleasure Chest. It is a single-story building just off the highway heading west out of town. I don't know why it's located so far from the traffic of downtown, but there never seems to be a lack of vehicles in the parking lot. People like their sex toys, and this place has everything imaginable.

As soon as we stroll through the heavy steel door, it takes a moment for our eyes to adjust to the soft glow from the overhead lights. Directly in front of us is a display featuring a scantily clad mermaid perched next to an open treasure chest filled with dildos and vibrators of every size, shape, and color imaginable. We give a quick wave to the twenty something female with a septum piercing and pixie cut behind the counter. My feet carry me down an aisle to the right side of the checkout counter. Dildos cover the plaster wall from floor to ceiling, some with accessories and others so discreet they can fit in your panties, and no one would suspect a thing.

This shopping trip is just what I need. I'm not a prude by any means, my nightstand drawer has a few basic battery-operated toys, but today's mission is to find something more adventurous.

"Oh, look at this one." Parisa holds up a realistic flesh colored dildo. "It has ten swirling and vibrating functions and a power boost."

Olivia looks over Parisa's shoulder to read the description. "And hands free with those suction cups. Things could get weird if the suction gives out. You're all heavily into your fantasy, going at it, and the suction releases. It's like the guys dick falls off and is now lodged inside of you."

All of us fall into a fit of laughter.

"That's kinda morbid. Only you would think of something like that," I say through my giggles.

"Have you never watched *Sex Sent Me to the ER*? That shit is scary. A fake penis stuck in your vagina is on the low priority end of the spectrum." Olivia reaches for another box on the wall. "How about this one? It has a handle so you can wield it like a sword." Olivia makes jabbing motions with the boxed dildo.

We continue our way around the perimeter of the store until we come up to the lingerie. I grab a lacy number off the rack and hold it up. "I don't understand the purpose of this one. Obviously, it leaves nothing to the imagination." All the straps crisscross across the front and back. "I would not only get tangled trying to put this on but also taking it off. That would not be a sexy sight." I contort my body on how it might look if I was wearing this contraption.

"Parisa, you could get this for Seth." Olivia tosses her the box.

A laugh springs from Parisa. "I bet he already has one in every color."

I move to her side to inspect the box. Inside sits a cock ring with a vibrating purple bowtie at the top. "Oh yeah, I bet he has a whole drawer full of those." Another round of laughter escapes us.

We stroll up and down the interior aisles and find a wide variety of lube ranging from flavored to organic. The next aisle shelves ticklers, restraints, and sex swings. At the end features all the sexual gag gifts you find at bachelor and bachelorette parties. Including all the various penis, boob, and vagina shaped trinkets imaginable. I'm tossing items into my basket as I shop around.

"You guys, I found it." I stare starry eyed at the wall in front of me. The holy grail of dildos. Something about it just spoke to me. The Clit Tickler Rabbit Vibrator. Olivia and Parisa come running to where I'm standing. "For a thumping good time." I point to the description on the box.

The girl behind the counter shouts, "Over three-hundred thousand of those have sold."

Well, let's make that three-hundred thousand and one.

Something is still missing. I wanted something daring and bold. As I round the corner, the toe of my shoe catches the edge of an endcap. My arms windmill as I stumble forward. Catching my balance before I end up face first into the floor, I look up and see it. A whole display of Booty Twinkle Anal Plugs. I'm looking for something bold, daring, something that says I can step outside my box, and this would be it.

Olivia and Parisa stride up to me flanking me on each side. Olivia says, "Girl, you are in for one hell of a ride. But you'll need this." She drops a bottle of anal lube into my basket. "It works better than regular lube. Trust me."

Turning the bag upside down, a plethora of vibrators, dildos, and lube tumble out on to my bed. I felt like I was in a money machine. Grabbing anything and everything I could get my hands on. As I'm closely inspecting my new purchases, my phone vibrates next to me. Looking at the screen, I see it's a message on FLIRT. I open the app and read the message.

Adonis21: Hey SexKitten. Yeah, I'm not letting that one go. Hope you had a good week.

Emberella55: *Groaning* I'm going to regret that name for the rest of my life. Also, I had a great week. After thinking about it and chatting with one of my girlfriends I'm doing it. No more guys.

Adonis21: Girlfriend? Are you becoming a lesbian? Can I watch?

Emberella55: HA! No, and if I was, still no. I just want to focus on myself and do things for me.

Adonis21: I'm still disappointed in the lesbian thing.

Emberella55: Of course you are. But this is important to me. I've always had a guy in my life, so I just want to learn how to live by myself.

Adonis21: So, on those cold and lonely nights with no guy around…

Emberella55: *Sends picture* I got it covered. *Wink*

Adonis21: Wow! I'll say! You got yourself covered for each day of the week.

Emberella55: Who masturbates every day of the week? Do you?

Adonis21: Pleads the fifth.

Emberella55: Show me your palms.

Adonis21: *Sends picture* See no hairy palms for me.

Emberella55: Oh, you have very nice hands. Do you get manicures?

Adonis21: No. But my sister bought me this lotion that works wonders.

Emberella55: Lotion, huh? You sure it's just for your hands?

Adonis21: Wouldn't you like to know. Okay, so let's go back to this picture. What's the spread?

Emberella55: Oh, you know just your standard vibrators. A dildo or two.

Adonis21: What's the shiny thing?

Emberella55: Oh, that…

Adonis21: Don't be getting all shy on me now.

Emberella55: Just thought maybe I would try something new.

Hitting send, my hands fly to my face as heat flares up my neck even though he can't see me. I can't believe I just told him that. He's going to think I'm some kinky sex nymphomaniac.

Adonis21: I like it.

I like it. *I like it.* That's all he has to say?

Emberella55: That's all you have to say?

Adonis21: Not sure what you want me to say…

Adonis21: SexKitten, do you like anal?

Well, I wasn't expecting that.

Emberella55: Whoa! Much like the act, I think that's a question you work up to.

Adonis21: Question avoidance. I'll take that as a yes.

I can't believe I'm chatting about anal sex with this stranger. Well, not a complete stranger. God, I feel like I've known him for years and we've only been chatting for a few weeks. But it has been almost every day. Even if it's a simple hi.

Emberella55: That's very presumptuous of you.

Adonis21: Well, which one are you going to test drive tonight?

Emberella55: Wouldn't you like to know?

Adonis21: Yes, yes, I would. That's why I asked the question. I need to make sure I have my visuals correct while I think about this later.

Is he going to think about me pleasuring myself, while he's pleasuring himself?

Adonis21: Or pictures work even better. Guys are visual creatures. *winking face emoji*

Adonis21: I'll start. *sends picture*

Enlarging the picture, I stare at a man lying in bed, the ambient light of the evening sun cascading up his body. The angle of the photo is pointing downward, starting with his sculpted chest. Next, my eyes gaze down his rippling six-pack abs, down his dark colored happy trail that leads me to a hint of his V. A white sheet is bunched at his hips. His other hand, not holding the camera, dips down into the sheet, covering a huge bulge. Is he… masturbating? All sorts of naughty thoughts flash through my mind. I envision myself tracing a feather light trail down his chest with my finger. Then through the small patch of dark chest hair. Running my tongue over every dip and curve of his abs. Kissing down the trail from his belly button to his waist. My phone dings, pulling me from my fantasy.

Adonis21: Are you staring? Drooling? Maybe touching yourself?

Emberella55: Someone thinks very highly of himself. But how do I know this is really you and not some picture you took from the internet? Write the date on a piece of paper and take another picture with the date. I see this on buy/sell sites all the time.

Adonis21: This feels like a meat market and I'm about to be auctioned off to the highest bidder.

Emberella55: Don't be silly. But I bet I could make a small fortune off these photos.

Several minutes pass until a new picture pops up with a handwritten date in the picture.

Adonis21: There. Happy?

Emberella55: Very
Adonis21: Like what you see?

Emberella55: *Wipes drool* It's alright.

Adonis21: Hahaha alright? You wound me.

Emberella55: *Saves picture for later* Oh, come on. You know you're hot.

Adonis21: How hot? Am I making you wet?

Emberella55: If you have to ask a girl if you're making her wet, you're doing it wrong.

Adonis21: Hahaha Well, if I were there, I wouldn't have to ask. I would just find out for myself.

Emberella55: Let's just say I had to put on a new pair of panties. *winking face emoji*

Adonis21: *Groans* I am going to have some pleasant dreams tonight.

Emberella55: You and me both.

Emberella55: Speaking of dreams. It's getting late. I should probably get going.

Adonis21: Alright. Sweet dreams.

Emberella55: You too. Night.

CHAPTER ELEVEN

What's the problem then?

Bennett

"So, how's the dating app going?" Liana looks at me from her beach lounger like a toddler who has a question to ask.

Looking down at my imaginary watch, I lift my head to meet her gaze. "Wow, I can't believe it only took you two hours before you asked." I take a swig of my cold beer and dig my toes into the cooling sand. The crisp sea salt smell wisps around me as the sun dips below the horizon.

"Well, you know, I didn't want to seem too eager." She winks at me.

Every year we take a family vacation to spend quality time together because Sunday dinner is not enough. My grandparents bought a condo in Siesta Key years ago. It's been passed down to each generation as a family getaway spot.

After the stress of selling the five-hundred-acre property and everything happening with Charlie, I needed to take some time to get my head on straight. Granted, this wasn't the break I wanted, but I'll take what I can.

"You're not very good at hiding it," I say.

"Stop stalling, I want to know all the things."

"What do you want to know?" Mark interrupts as he sits in the chair next to Liana as their two kids run past us to splash around on the shoreline.

Turning to her husband, Liana says, "Oh, just about these women my baby brother has falling for him."

"Well, I don't know about that." I reach into the cooler and pass Mark a beer.

"So humble. How could they not fall for you? You're so adorable." She reaches over to try and pinch my cheeks, but I smack her hand away.

"You may be older, but I am stronger." Looking over at Mark, I ask, "How do you put up with this?" I point to my sister. "This is why I'm single."

Mark laughs. "Yeah, I wonder about that myself."

An oomph escapes Mark as Liana backhands him in the chest. He rubs the sore spot and we all burst out laughing.

Turning her attention back to me, Liana asks, "No, in all seriousness, what's happening? Find anyone?"

Fighting back a smile and failing miserably, I say, "There's one girl I've been talking to."

A teenage squeal leaves my sister as she sits up straighter. "Tell me everything!"

"There's not much to tell." I downplay the situation. "I met a girl and we've been chatting here and there. Nothing serious." I take another drink of my beer for fear I might spill the whole situation to her.

"Are you going to meet? Oh, bring her over for Sunday dinner!" Liana squeals with delight.

"Yeah, that's just what I need. Invite her over and introduce her to the crazy family. That sounds like a great idea."

"If she can prove she can hang with us, then she's a keeper."

Liana turns toward Mark. "Right, honey? I invited you

over for Sunday dinner and when you didn't run screaming, I just knew you were the one."

"Wasn't Mark in the bathroom for a really long time? Probably trying to figure out a way to escape through the window," I counter.

"I contemplated if a broken leg from the two-story drop would be worth it. In the end, I sucked it up and took one for the team. The team being all the other guys out there." Mark winks at Liana.

Mark and I burst out laughing while Liana narrows her eyes at her husband.

"Haha. If it wasn't for me, you would have ended up with what's her name…" She trails off, trying to think of the name.

"Sheila Peterson," Mark says with a shudder.

"Yes! She was always trying to get with you and would have eventually worn you down. So, I saved you. Remember that. Bennett, didn't she try hooking up with you too?"

"I don't think there was a guy on campus she didn't try to get with, and I was two years younger than her. Wonder what ever happened to her?"

Liana sits back in her chair. "The last I heard she was living a couple towns over and married to husband number three."

We sit in silence for a few moments. The hypnotic sound of the waves lapping against the shore fills my head with thoughts of Charlie. Why can't I get this girl out of my head? When I wake up, she's the first thing I think about. When I close my eyes, she's the last thing I see. Suddenly, the screeching of seagulls and kids screaming pulls me from my thoughts. Liana gets up to see what all the commotion is about as Mark moves to take the empty seat next to me.

"You know your sister just wants you happy. You've spent so many years of your life taking care of this family. She would love to see you start one of your own."

"Yeah, yeah. Someday, but it hasn't been a top priority of

mine. I scored that big deal at work, so that solidified my future with the company. So now I'll just wait and see what comes next."

I watch as my sister wrangles her two little kids as they squeal with delight and wonder how she does it with such ease. I can't help but smile; maybe I do want that. A family of my own.

"Well, this girl I was talking about. It's a little more complicated than what it seems." I confess the whole situation with Charlie and FLIRT and how we work together. But that I can't stop thinking about her and how much a crave her.

After my word vomit, Mark picks up his beer and takes a long pull. "Huh, that complicates things a little. But let me ask you this. Is there anything that says co-workers can't date?"

"I'm not her direct superior, so no it wouldn't be against company policy."

"So, what's the problem, then? If you like her, you need to go for it. If you don't, you'll never know if she's the one." As Mark gazes upon his wife playing with their kids. "If I didn't take the bet with Liana, I wouldn't be where I'm at today. Kissing her made me realized my true feelings."

What's the problem then? I let his question stew in my head for a few minutes. Well, that's a good question. She hated me but seemed to get over that when she kissed me. But now the big question would be how will she react when she finds out I'm Adonis21?

CHAPTER TWELVE

They are not penises

Charlie

"I bring you gifts." I place a decorative bag stuffed with tissue paper in front of Olivia. She looks up from her desk to inspect the bag.

"Gifts! I love gifts!" Olivia squeals as she dives into the bag. Pulling out the four rectangle shaped items, her brows squish together. "You got me…" She places each item up right in front of her. "Knitted penises?"

"No. They're potholders. I knitted them myself." I hold my head high.

"They look like penises. Especially this flesh colored one." Olivia inspects the homemade items before tossing them back into the bag.

"They are not penises. They are potholders."

"What's not a penis?" Parisa asks while walking up to the desk.

Olivia tosses her one of the knitted potholders. A splitting grin covers her face. "Here, have a penis."

"It's not a penis," I groan.

"It kinda looks like a penis," Parisa nods.

"Keep it. I have three more." Olivia holds up her bag, giving it a shake.

"Did someone say penis?" A male voice cuts in.

When I look up, Trey is standing on the other side of the desk, and I'm surprised to see Bennett standing next to him. He's been out of the office all week. When I checked his online work calendar it said he was on vacation, which meant I couldn't talk to him about the kiss.

"Why yes they did." Olivia digs into her bag and whips out two potholders and tosses them to the guys. "Presents for you."

Trey inspects it before holding it down by his crotch. "Is this a sweater for my dick? If so, it might be kinda small." He sticks his fingers inside, trying to stretch out the yarn.

Covering my face I mumble, "They're potholders. Why would I make a sweater for your penis? You know what, don't answer that." Uncovering my eyes, it's just Trey. Bennett has disappeared.

"Thanks for the dick warmer." Trey wiggles it in the air as he walks away.

Olivia turns her attention back to me. "You know I love my penises or potholders, as you call them, and all the other things you have DIYed for my apartment." Olivia wiggles the potholder in my direction. "And I know you said you were taking time for yourself, but maybe it's time to see what's out there again. I just don't think you're going to be the next Martha Stewart."

"I love my mason jar candle holders. They match so well with my painted plant pots. For all the plants I'll kill. At least they'll look pretty when they die." Parisa tries to surpass a giggle but fails when Olivia cracks up next to her.

For the past couple of weeks, I've busied myself with every Pinterest project I could find. Some of the finished products turned out better than say, these knitted pen—potholders. But on top of the crafting, I've been doing some real self-discovery, which included going out to dinner at a restaurant by myself. I'll admit it was slightly awkward at first because I thought everyone was staring at me but in reality, they weren't. They probably didn't even care but I decided to not stay for dessert and instead went home and started my next craft project to give to my friends.

"I hate you guys." Pouting, I cross my arms over my chest.

"Charlie, we love you. And we know you're just finding ways to distract yourself, but no more. Seriously, no more," Olivia states.

"I agree, it's time to get back on that horse and find yourself a cowboy." Parisa mimics throwing a lasso.

"Did I just fail at this whole being single thing?"

Rubbing my back, Olivia replies, "Oh no, honey. You did great."

"So great," Parisa chimes in.

"There are just some people who can live alone and others who can't. You are the latter," Olivia says.

Burying my face in my hands, I sigh before looking back up. "I don't know if I should be thrilled that I have best friends who are so honest or feel so pathetic because I need the company of a guy in my life."

"There is nothing wrong with not wanting to be alone. We all need love and affection in our lives. Being far away from your own family, it can be hard to get that. You spent time finding yourself and your love of… phallus shaped crafts…" Everyone giggles as Olivia holds up the potholder.

"So, tonight will be 'Charlie's reunited into the world of dating' night! We'll go out and have drinks at Porter's and see where the night takes us," Olivia exclaims.

A ping from my work email draws my attention. I click open and begin reading.

Charlie,

Please come to my office as soon as possible.

Bennett

Blinking rapidly, I read the words over again. Oh shit. Bennett never sends me ominous emails like this. Add the fact I've hardly seen him or spoken to him since the night of the kiss, sends a twinge of nausea coursing through my body. He was away on vacation, then he was held up in his office or out to meetings with clients. Even today, when he was with Trey, he didn't say a word. I close my eyes and inhale a calming breath. Without any further delay, I stand and wipe away the invisible lint on my skirt and let Olivia know Bennett has summoned me to his office.

The elevator ride up is only one floor, but it feels like twenty. My heart is beating through my chest, unsure of what he has to say. It was a wonderful kiss. It's been on replay in my dreams every night. But it was inappropriate and should have never happened. And it can't happen ever again. Even though I wouldn't complain if it did.

Stopping in front of his closed door, I wipe my palms on my skirt. A bead of sweat trickles down my back. Everything will be fine. I repeat the saying as if it's my mantra. When I've collected my thoughts, I raise my hand and gently knock.

A deep baritone voice sounds from the other side. Slowly, I turn the knob and poke my head through the opening. The afternoon sun shines through the large window behind him, framing a much better view of the city than expected since the building sits on a hill. A hopeful glint flares behind his blue eyes as his lips quirk up to the side with the slightest hint of a smile.

"You wanted to see me?"

"Yes. Please come in. Close the door and have a seat." Bennett stands and directs me to the chair in front of his desk.

He clears his throat. "How are you doing?"

Why does this feel like the awkward morning after a one-night stand? This is just uncomfortable for all parties involved. Not really sure where he is going with this, I offer a hesitant reply, "Okay…"

He fidgets with the paperwork sitting in front of him. "Good, good. Let me just cut to the chase. About that night a few weeks ago outside Porter's. I just wanted to say—"

Cutting him off before he can say anything else, I blurt out, "I am so sorry about that night. It was not appropriate. We work together. I was in this completely vulnerable state after breaking up with my cheating boyfriend and you were just being so kind and I just… I don't know. Went for it. And I know it was completely wrong and I'm sorry. And it will never happen again." Finally taking a breath, I look up and see a wide-eyed Bennett staring back at me.

Hesitancy laces his voice. "Oh good… Well, now that we've cleared that up, we can just go on with business as usual. Just two people working together."

"Yes. Sounds like an excellent plan. We'll just put all that behind us. Pretend it never happened." I release a low chuckle.

"Yes, never happened," Bennett says in a clipped tone. He stands and steps back from behind his desk. My gaze travels from his long legs in his tailored suit pants, up his torso to where his pristine white button-down dress shirt hugs his sculpted chest and large biceps. I continue my gawking as I reach his face and the light scruff that covers his cheeks and jaw. A weak smile plays on his lips. When my eyes meet his, thoughts from that night flit through my mind and heat creeps up my cheeks. His smile grows larger, making his dimple pop. Can he sense how much I enjoyed that kiss and how much I want it to happen again? Quickly looking away before he can read more of my dirty thoughts, I stand up and his large six-foot-five frame towers over my five-foot-six with heels.

Clearing my throat. "Well, if that is all. I should really get back to work. Glad we could clear all that up. "

"Me too, Charlie. Have a good rest of your day."

Offering him a weak smile, I make my way out of his office and back toward the elevators. Once inside, I lean against the wall, close my eyes, and wonder what the hell just happened.

Later that night, I'm scrolling through the home page of Netflix, wanting to find my next binge watch. I think back to earlier today. Olivia and Parisa think I should try dating again and maybe it's time. Anything with Bennett is off the table. Then my mind drifts to Adonis21. I haven't heard from him in a while. Should I just text him? Just then, my phone chimes next to me, and I see the heart icon of the FLIRT app. A smile plays on my lips as my heart rate speeds up. My fingers fumble as I open the app. Excitement courses through my body at the thought of talking to him again. But that's short lived when I don't see his name, but a different one.

LifeOnTheGreen: Just wanted to say you look beautiful in your picture.

CHAPTER THIRTEEN

I'm not moving on yet

Bennett

"Man, I fucked up." I take a swig of my beer and look at Trey for answers. The noise of music and people hollering flutter around a packed Porter's.

"You didn't strike while the iron was hot. I always thought you were a better closer than that."

"That's shitty advice." I place my now empty bottle on the bar and signal for the bartender.

"I can't be your relationship whisperer when I don't do relationships."

"Clearly," I deadpan. "I should've just stopped her before she blurted out that it was a mistake."

"Shoulda. Coulda. Woulda."

I side-eye Trey and his terrible advice.

"Well, the good news is there is a plethora of women here tonight and I'm sure you can have your pick. I'll even give you first dibs." Trey clasps my shoulder and swivels his stool around. "Over there. By the pool table. An entire group of beautiful girls. I'm sure one of them must be single."

I turn to Trey as he winks and flashes a dimpled smile at one of the girls. "Do you ever tire of the single life? Like, maybe it's time to settle down?"

"Has your sister gotten in your head again? Why would I want to give this up? No strings. No commitments. All that other stuff is not for me, man. I am perfectly happy, just like this. But what are you going to do? Sulk and pine after a girl who has written you off as a mistake. This is a prime opportunity to get that girl out of your head and get a new one in your bed."

"You're so fucking poetic."

"Just call me Treyspeare." He winks.

I take a few minutes to let Trey's words stew in my head. Maybe he's right. She was pretty quick to brush off everything that happened between us. If she's over it and moving on, then maybe I should, too.

The bartender sets a beer down in front of me. "You know what, let's make that a whiskey sour."

"Fuck yes! My bro is back!"

Trey is leaning over the pool table behind a petite blonde, giving her a lesson on how to properly hit the cue ball. I'm sure he is rubbing his dick all over her ass based on the little giggles she releases. In the meantime, a curvy brunette is standing between my open legs, rambling on about her cat and all the cute things he does. Newsflash, I don't care that he stands up on his hind legs and looks like a squirrel for a treat. Each time her hand caresses my chest or rubs on my thigh, my mind drifts to Charlie and the night of the infamous kiss. How her delicate hands touched me and caressed me. At that thought, my cock grows hard.

"Do you have any pets?" Her question pulls me from my thoughts.

"Oh uh, no. Got too much going on to care for any."

"That's why I like cats. They pretty much take care of themselves." Her fingers dance near the crotch of my jeans and brushes against my growing erection. Her eyes twinkle with delight.

Sorry sweetheart, that's not because of you.

"If you'll excuse me. I'm going to go use the restroom." Gently directing her from between my legs, I stand. I push my way through the crowd of people to get to the restrooms on the other side of the bar. After washing my hands and stepping out the door, I'm pushed back inside by a hard thrust. Surprised, I'm shoved up against the wood planked wall. Before I know it, the brunette's arms wrap around my neck and her lips press to mine. It takes a second to realize what's happening. Finally collecting my bearings, I grip her shoulders and push her off me. A whine escapes her lips. The lust in her eye quickly turns to disappointment as she realizes she's not about to get lucky.

"Sorry if I gave you the wrong impression, but this isn't going to happen in a men's bathroom."

"Well, we can also go back to my place," she purrs while stepping closer with her hand on my chest, a pointy fingernail drawing lazy circles.

"I mean, this isn't going to happen at all."

Dropping her hand. "Oh. You're such an asshole!" She shoves me. Hard. Then turns around and rips the door open and stomps out. The door slams shut with a bang, and I take a second to digest what happened.

This is why I should stay away from barflies.

I open the door, looking both ways to make sure crazy cat lady isn't hiding in the shadows ready to pounce again. Luckily, the hallway is empty. I stroll back to the other side to find Trey with the blonde's tongue down his throat. So much for being my wingman. The blonde finally lets him up for oxygen and I give him a wave, so he knows I'm taking off. He tosses me a head nod before giving the blonde his undivided attention again. So apparently, I'm not moving on yet.

CHAPTER FOURTEEN

There is no competition

Bennett

Two months later

I straighten some papers on my desk when a loud grumble sounds from my stomach. Peering down at my watch, I see it's almost two p.m. Where has the time gone? My office door flies open and Trey strides in with Seth close behind.

"Don't you knock? I could've had a client in here."

"Knocking's not my style. Plus, I checked your calendar, and it was empty. We're hungry. We should go get a bite to eat before we call it a day." Trey plops down in the chair across from my desk while Seth takes the one next to him. Trey points to Seth. "And this guy looked like he needed a break from Parisa."

Seth bobs his head up and down. "The insistent tapping of her pen on her desktop would drive any man insane. And she doesn't even know she's doing it. Just tap, tap, tap all day long."

I bark out a laugh. "Let's go."

I'm about to stand up when Seth asks, "So you never told

me what happened between you and Charlie. There was the kiss, but then what? The past few months you've been distant and always leaving out the backdoor whenever possible. You used to love riling that girl up."

I let out a sigh.

"He pussied out," Trey interrupts. "Now, let's go get some food and you two girls can gossip later."

"What I was trying to say…" I glare at Trey while he huffs as he sits back down in his chair. "After the kiss, life got a little hectic. When I finally had a moment to digest everything, I asked to see her in my office only for her to tell me it was a mistake."

"So that's it? You're not going to do anything?" Seth asks.

"Not a damn thing. Now food. Let's go." Trey stands and strolls toward the door.

"I'm going to feel sorry for the woman who ends up with your dumbass." Seth stands and shoves Trey's shoulder.

"Then you'll feel sorry for no one because that love bullshit isn't for me." Trey holds up two fingers. "Two weeks, that's my limit. After that, they want to spend the night and then you find their toothbrush in your bathroom and then suddenly you have new flowery throw pillows on your couch. Next thing you know, she is moving all her shit in. Your closet space is now a tiny sliver on the far side. Then you have to switch which side of the bed you sleep on because she doesn't like sleeping on the side next to the door because what if someone breaks into the house in the middle of the night. Being on the side closest to the door means she would be the first person the intruder would encounter, hence the first one to be murdered. But guess what? I don't want to get murdered either."

"So, you know all this from experience?" Seth asks sarcastically.

I shake my head at Seth. "Don't ask. There are not enough beers to survive that conversation."

Trey is halfway to the elevator, mumbling to himself about women and never settling down. Seth grips my shoulder, halting my progress. When I turn to him, he asks, "So Charlie, you're just going to let it go?"

"Honestly, I don't know. I thought she was into it but calling it a mistake tells me otherwise. Seems like a waste of time to pursue something that will never happen."

Seth just nods and then we continue our way to the elevators. By the time we catch up with Trey, he's already downstairs slathering on the charm with Olivia and Charlie.

As we approach the reception desk, I overhear part of their conversation about drinks tonight at Porter's. We make our way towards the front. I offer a quick greeting to Olivia and Charlie, but I can't take my focus off Charlie. Her hair is tied back with a loose strand that falls, framing her face. I want to reach over and tuck it behind her ear, so I have a full view of her beautiful face and her sparkling hazel eyes with tiny flecks of gold that dance in her irises. My gaze lingers to the silver chain around her slender neck and dips into the cleavage of her button-down blouse.

Just then, Trey's voice pulls me out of my daydream. "So, drinks tonight."

"Jake is trying something new at the bar and is having a live band perform. We want to show our support," Olivia says.

"And Seth, put on something more appropriate for the ladies. This bow tie just doesn't do it." Trey reaches over to straighten Seth's bow tie, but Seth knocks his hand away.

"You would be surprised how many ladies actually like the bow tie." Seth smiles.

"It's kinda cute, and the black rimmed glasses. He has the nerdy Clark Kent thing going on," Olivia says.

Trey stands up taller and brushes a hand down the lapel of his black Armani suit jacket. "So, you're telling me you would rather have Clark Kent over Superman?"

I bark out a laugh. "Dude, Clark Kent is Superman."

"And he just proved my point." Seth clasps Trey on the shoulder.

"Whatever, man." Trey shrugs him off and shifts towards Olivia and Charlie. "Drinks eight p.m. See you ladies there."

I give them both a tight smile and a nod as I walk toward the exit. Friday bar night with the guys. Fun. Friday bar night with the girl who dismissed me faster than a housewife not getting an enormous kitchen island in her new house. Fucking miserable.

Porter's is wall to wall bodies. I spot Olivia, Parisa, and Trey along the back wall. Luckily, they got here early to snag us a table. Snaking my way through the crowd, I wave to Jake behind the bar as he slings drinks.

"Wow, this place is getting crazy. Looks like there will be a great turnout." I pull out a stool across from Trey and Olivia.

"Hey man, you finally made it. Didn't know it was going to take you so long to put your face on," Trey remarks.

"Yeah, good one, when you're one who spends an hour on your hair." I raise my hand to mess up his perfectly styled hair, but he ducks away just in time.

"Hey, hey, no touching. That's only for the ladies to touch and usually they are riding—"

Olivia cuts Trey off. "Stop! No one wants to hear that!"

"Are you sure? I don't quite hear the conviction in your voice. I bet you would like to know exactly how it feels." Trey winks at Olivia.

"You two need to fuck already. This back and forth of 'I want to stab you one minute, rip your clothes off the next' glances you give each other is getting old," Parisa says from next to me.

"Oh, so just like you and Seth." Trey quirks an eyebrow at her.

"No. I just want to stab him," Parisa deadpans.

Olivia turns to Parisa. "Don't you have to go to that conference with him that's coming up? "

"Don't remind me. I just hope his room is on the opposite side of the hotel as mine," Parisa replies.

Charlie strides toward the table, her brown locks cascade down the front of her shoulders. Her tan off the shoulder dress hugs her tits perfectly. She glances in my direction. Her eyes light up like the North Star and a wide smile spreads across her face. A grin pulls at my lips. With each step, she gets closer and my heart beats faster with each passing second. I push my chair back to stand, but she flounces past me. My gaze trails in the direction she's moving but stops when her arms wrap around some guy's neck. *Maybe it's her brother?*

Then he cups her face and places a soft kiss on her lips.

Okay, not her brother.

She saunters back to the table, her fingers intertwined with his.

"Hey everyone, this is Kaleb. Kaleb, this is everyone." She waves her hand around the table. The girls get all giddy and start gushing over the new guy.

Who the hell is he and where did he come from?

Trey leans over and whispers over my shoulder. "He seems like a tool. Zero competition."

Turning toward Trey, I say, "There is no competition."

"That's the right attitude to have. Be confident."

"No, I mean, there is no competition. There is nothing happening between us."

Why do I feel like that is the biggest lie I ever told myself?

"Yeah, okay, whatever you say, man." Trey picks up his beer and takes a pull and I do the same.

Charlie and Kaleb turn towards me, and I give them the

biggest, fakest smile I can muster. *Maybe I should tone is down a notch.* So instead, I offer a half smile with a nod. "Hey man, nice to meet you. I'm Bennett and this is Trey," I say, pointing in his direction.

"Nice to meet you guys. Charlie has told me a lot about everyone," Kaleb says.

I watch as Kaleb pulls Charlie's chair out and offers her the seat. He whispers something in her ear and her cheeks turn a dusty rose. Then he slowly caresses her face and tucks a strand of hair behind her ear, and she looks at him like he's the only man in the world. Clearly, I'm just the gum stuck to the bottom of her shoe.

"Well, how about some shots? Anyone want some shots?" I shove my chair from the table and trample toward the bar before anyone can answer me. Why am I here? I should just leave. Say an emergency came up. That would be better than torturing myself by watching Charlie with that guy all night. Trey saddles up next to me at the bar. The noise around us picks up as the rock band, Onyx Stone, starts their sound check.

Leaning in so he doesn't have to yell over the noise, he says, "So nothing's happening between you two, right?" Trey flashes me a cocky smirk. I shake my head at him. If Trey wasn't my best friend, I would punch him in his smug face.

After a few minutes, the bartender comes our way. "Two shots of Patron," I shout to her.

"Thanks, man. It's been a while since I've had tequila. I better get the training wheels"

"No, these are mine. Get your own, asshole."

"Hey, same team. I'm just pointing out what you already know but are trying to deny."

I take down the two shots like a man in need of water in the desert. When we make it back to the table, the band has started playing and Charlie and dick face are nowhere in sight.

"Where did everyone go?" Trey asks.

"Dance floor. Why? You want to join? I want to see what kinda moves you got." Olivia winks at Trey.

"I don't need a dance floor to show you want kinda moves I got, sweetheart."

"I think I'm going to be sick," Parisa mutters while pretending to gag.

I take a seat, my view directly toward the dance floor, and within seconds, I spot the two lovebirds dancing away. Kaleb holds her hand as he twirls her. Her skirt flaring out with each turn and her chestnut locks flowing behind. Her smile lighting up her face even in the dim light. This is torture and I need more tequila. After a few more songs and several more tequila shots, Charlie and fuck stick make their way back to the table.

"Well, looks like you guys have been partying without us," Charlie says with a chuckle.

"It's a bar, with a band. What else did you expect?" I deadpan, then direct my attention to the douche canoe. "So, what kind of work do you do, Kaleb?"

Kaleb squares his shoulders and stands tall. "I'm a Junior Sales Executive for a power sports company."

"Just a Junior, huh? Like a glorified manager?" I eye up the man standing in front of me while Charlie, standing next to him, looks like she's ready to kill me.

"Uh, well, I guess that's one way to put it. But I hear a Senior position will open soon, so I have my eye on that," Kaleb says.

"Oh honey, you didn't tell me that. You'd be great." Charlie beams up at him.

Kaleb wraps his arm around Charlie's shoulders. "Well, I didn't want to say anything to jinx it."

"Well, too late, you just did," I murmur under my breath, but not quite enough for Charlie not to hear. She narrows her eyes at me.

"I'm parched. Let's go get a drink." Charlie grabs Kaleb's hand and intertwines her delicate fingers with his as they prance off to the bar.

The innocent gesture feels like a rope is strangling my heart. My gaze lingers on her as she disappears into the crowd. Dammit, I'm such an asshole. She doesn't deserve my piss poor attitude. She's done nothing wrong. It's not her fault I didn't man up when I had the chance and make her mine, and now she's moved on. Swallowing the last of my beer, I slam my glass back down on the table a little harder than normal. Everyone looks my way, silence taking over the table. "I'm going to take off." I push my stool back and stand. Before anyone can say anything, I turn and walk towards the exit. I spare one last glance towards the bar and at that exact moment Charlie turns around. Our eyes connect for a few beats before I turn back and shove my way out the door.

CHAPTER FIFTEEN

I don't need you trying to play matchmaker

Bennett

It's been two days since the bar incident. Two days where I was a complete jackass for no other reason than jealousy. I had my chance and let it slip through my fingers.

I swing my mallet against a rusty axle on an antique wheelbarrow for a neighbor down the road. All the hammering has been a great way to release this pent-up frustration. I tried it Trey's way and went out with a couple of women, but I wasn't in the right head space. I would feel like a dick leading them on knowing it wouldn't go anywhere. My phone buzzing on the wooden stool next to me alerts me to a text message. Glancing over to see who it's from, I roll my eyes and dismiss the message. A few seconds later, my phone vibrates again. And then again. And again. Without delay, my ring tone sounds, and I know I can no longer avoid it.

Pressing the talk button, I answer. "What do you want?"

"Is that how you greet your sister?"

"Only when I really don't want to talk."

"Well tough. You know, if you didn't answer, I was just going to come over."

"Yep. Now what do you want? I'm kinda busy here." I've been doing anything and everything to stay busy this weekend, so I don't think about… *her*.

"Sorry Mr. I'm too busy to talk to your sister. Your only sister, by the way."

"Yeah, yeah, get on with it."

"You're still coming over for Sunday dinner, right?"

"Have I ever not made it?"

"Okay good. Be here by six p.m. Oh and wear the blue Eton button-up shirt you have. That will look super nice. Kay, Bye!"

"Liana. Liana." Dead air fills the other end. I stare down at the screen and the call has ended. What the fuck? Why am I dressing up for Sunday dinner? I never dress up for Sunday dinner.

Then it dawns on me.

She's setting me up.

I shift into park, my hands still gripping the steering wheel as I take a minute to myself. I'm contemplating either killing my sister or killing my sister. Murder wasn't on my to-do list for today but sometimes plans can change. Why would she think I'd want to be set up? Especially after all the bullshit with Charlie. I finish cursing my sister and make my way towards the front door. Before I can raise my hand to turn the knob, the front door flies open.

"Uncle Bennett!" My niece and nephew scream at the top of their lungs as each hugs a leg.

"Hey kiddos! Where's your mom?" I may just need to kill her. Before they can give me a response, they're off running in the opposite direction.

"Oh, Bennett! You're here," my sister beams. "And you're

wearing my favorite shirt. This one always looked so good on you." Liana reaches up to straighten my collar.

I knock her hands away. "What the hell is going on here?"

"I have someone for you to meet."

"Yeah, that's what I was afraid of. I'm not doing this. I don't need you trying to play matchmaker." I reach for the doorknob, ready to get out of here, when Liana stops me.

"Matchmaker? What are you talking about? One of Mark's co-workers is interested in purchasing some property. He told her you were the best in the business. I didn't want you showing up looking like a hobo."

"Oh…"

"Yeah… oh. Did you think I was trying to set you up?" Liana laughs. "I know you're still hung up on Charlie. Mark filled me in." She shrugs her shoulders. "Which I'm surprised you never told me. But anyway, what kind of sister do you think I am?"

"Everyone else seems to tell me I need to move on."

"Who? Trey? He's always looking for his next piece of ass, so of course he's going to tell you to move on. That guy couldn't hold on to a relationship if it was velcroed to his ass. Don't take dating advice from him. So, let me introduce you to Sara and you can go do what you do best." Liana elbows me in the ribs. "But just in case, she's single and beautiful." She gives me a wink before walking up the stairs towards the kitchen.

After the little misunderstanding about Sara, the rest of the night went on without a hitch. We had dinner and a couple of drinks while Sara and I talked about what kind of property she was interested in. Besides that, conversation flowed easily with her. My sister was right. Sara is a very attractive woman. Unfortunately, every time I look into her eyes, I'm reminded of the same hazel ones that belong to Charlie.

CHAPTER SIXTEEN

Tequila. Make it a double

Charlie

"Girl, you look deep in thought." Olivia's voice pulls me from my head as I sit at my desk staring off into space.

Brushing it off. "Oh. Yeah, it's nothing."

"The way your face is scrunched up, it doesn't seem like nothing." Olivia raises a perfectly sculpted, questioning brow at me.

"Just thoughts from the weekend."

Friday night was awkward. I wasn't expecting Bennett to show up, so having Kaleb there put a weird vibe in the air. But I shouldn't feel guilty. Bennett means nothing to me. But I do. His behavior screamed of jealousy. But why? He can have any woman he wants, and he certainly likes to flaunt them in front of me anytime the opportunity arises, even though that hasn't happened in awhile. He agreed it would be best if we just remained co-workers. So, why is it when I start dating someone, he suddenly wants me? Talk about emotional whiplash.

Just as I'm about to lay it all out to Olivia, a delivery guy holding an enormous bouquet of red roses walks up to the desk. Before he can even set it down, both of us stand and Olivia is reaching for the card buried inside and passes it to me.

"Read it." She bounces back and forth on the balls of her feet.

I flip open the envelope flap and pull out the card. "Charlie, dinner tonight. I have something very important to talk to you about. Yours, Kaleb."

The card falls from my fingers and flutters to my desk.

Olivia squeals next to me. "Oh Em Gee! What do you think he has to talk to you about? Marriage seems a bit early. Move in together?"

Feeling dumbfounded, I pick up the card and flip it between my fingers looking for any type of clue for what he wants to talk about. "I'm not sure. We've only been together for a few months, so yeah, marriage would be a bit of a rush…"

"But you two are perfect together. You have so much in common. I would imagine it would head in that direction. You two would make such cute babies! Maybe he's just one of those guys who gets straight to the point." Olivia smiles with glee.

An unease settles in my stomach. Kaleb's amazing. I couldn't ask for a better man than him, but am I ready for marriage? I want to someday, but now? With Kaleb? Plopping down in my chair, I stare at a nonexistent spot on the far wall. All the while Olivia is animatedly telling Parisa about the card and flowers and something about babies.

"Charlie. Hello. Earth to Charlie." Olivia waves her hand in front of my face.

"Yeah, what's up?" Pulling my attention from the spot, I tilt my head up to look up at her.

"Everything alright? You don't seem very excited."

"Must have been those tacos from lunch not agreeing with me," I rub my stomach. The lie drips off my tongue.

"Let me grab you a bottle of water." Parisa quickly swivels on her heel to head toward the break room.

Olivia eyes me skeptically. "Are you sure it's the tacos or are you nervous about tonight?"

Just then Parisa returns with a water. I snag it from her hand and guzzle it down. Mostly, to buy myself a few extra seconds to compose myself. I should be excited. This is exciting news. He's going to ask me to move in. We are taking the next step in our relationship. Even after my little pep talk, I'm not one hundred percent feeling the excitement. But sometimes you just need to fake it.

With a grin plastered on my face. "So, who's helping me to get ready tonight?"

My reflection in the full-length mirror stares back at me. I tilt my head to the side, thinking this angle will make me feel better. *Nope, doesn't work*. I slant my head to the other side. *Not any better*. Now I just feel like a dog who perks their ears up and cocks their head to the side. An exasperated sigh leaves my lips as my butt hits the ottoman. Suddenly, the intercom sounds, pulling me from my self-pity. A few seconds after I buzz them up, Olivia is pushing her way through my door with a bottle of wine in her hands, Parisa trailing behind her with a second bottle.

"Your fairy godmothers are here and ready to make you look so damn hot Kaleb will want to rip your dress off and have his way with you right in the middle of the restaurant!" Olivia cheers with excitement.

Parisa grabs three wine glasses from the kitchen, knowing exactly where they were as if it was her own house. She hands me a full glass as she eyes my outfit. "You're not wearing that, are you?"

I look down at my olive-colored tunic tank dress and then back up to Parisa.

"What's wrong with this dress?"

"It does nothing to accentuate your assets. And you want all your assets accentuated tonight." Parisa winks and pulls me towards my second bedroom.

Forty-five minutes and a bottle and a half of wine later, I am looking good enough to eat, Olivia's words, and I'll be going to pound town tonight, Parisa's words. I shoo them both out the door before Kaleb arrives and catch my reflection in the mirror. The black scoop neck dress with the open back and black strappy pumps accentuates some assets. Smokey eye makeup and just a hint of lip gloss. I pluck my shawl and matching clutch from my shelf to finish off the ensemble. With one last glance in the mirror, I stand straight, shoulders back, feeling like I have all the confidence in the world. I start flaunting all my angles. Trying different poses. My nerves for tonight settling down because I know with one look, Kaleb won't be able to resist me. Just as I am blowing kisses to myself in the mirror a knock sounds on the door startling me while my clutch hits the floor.

"I'm coming!" I yell then realize how inappropriate that sounds. Releasing a chuckle, I regain my composure. I blame it on the wine.

When I pull the door open, my heart skips a beat. The man in front of me is looking dapper in his three-piece gray suit. This is the first time I've seen him dressed like this. I'm thinking forget dinner, we should just stay here and bang. When my eyes lock onto his, a smile pulls at his lips. I bring my hand up to my mouth, mostly to check for drool, when I am greeted with a full-blown smile, and I can't help but reciprocate.

"You. Look. Amazing." Kaleb eyes me from head to toe.

"Oh, this old thing." I give him a cheeky grin. "Come in." I move out of the doorway, giving him space to move inside.

"How did you get in? The main door is always locked." I close the door behind him.

"Parisa and Olivia held it open for me."

Before I can say anything else, he cuts me off by pulling me into his arms.

"I would love to just stay in..." He kisses my shoulder. "And slowly take this dress off you..." He kisses the nape of my neck. "And feather your entire body with kisses..." He kisses me again.

"Oh, I like this idea. Let's do that."

Kaleb chuckles against my sensitive skin. "After dinner. I have an important question for you. Then we can finish all this."

I let out a heavy, exaggerated sigh. "Fine. Dinner first. But let's make this quick. Maybe just appetizers."

I grab his hand and lead him toward the door. The sooner we get this dinner over with, the sooner we get to sexy times.

The car jolts to a stop in front of one of the most elegant restaurants in town, The Boat House. The last time I was here was when I caught Jared cheating.

I reach over and rest my hand on Kaleb's. "Are you sure you don't want to go somewhere else?"

"You don't like this place?"

Not wanting to rehash the whole ex-boyfriend situation, I just smile. "No. This place is fine."

Kaleb reciprocates with a smile of his own before he exits and strolls around the front of the car to open my door. I rest my hand in his as I step out. The young valet attendant greets Kaleb, apprehension apparent by his jerky movements. I feel the same way, kid. I link my arm with Kaleb's as we stride our way through the large wood doors. Instantly, the hostess greets us and escorts us to our table. Dimly lit sconces fill the room. Large half circle, high back booths line the perimeter. The hostess seats us at one in the back corner. The tea light candles on the table with the dark red drapery set up a seductive atmosphere. I scoot into the booth as Kaleb enters on the other side. We make quick work to order a bottle of wine and by the time our two glasses are placed on the table my nerves are getting the best of me again. I fidget in my seat while inspecting my nails and then grab for my glass of wine. *Would it be inappropriate to chug this?* I decide to keep it civil and take a sip, hoping to calm my nerves.

Kaleb reaches over to clasp my hand. "Hey, is everything okay? You seem nervous?"

"Oh, I'm great." My voice higher than normal. "This wine is delicious. Black cherry with just a hint of mocha. Don't you think?" I reach for my wine, taking another big gulp. Trying to play it cool but failing miserably. "So, you wanted to talk?"

"Well, I was hoping to wait until after dinner, but you seem like you might burst if I don't tell you now." Kaleb shifts his body towards mine and clasps my hands. "You know we've been together for about two months now and while that may not seem like a lot of time to some, I just knew the moment I connected with you that you were something special. I've loved every single moment we've spent together."

My eyes dart to his hand as it leaves mine and dips inside his suit jacket. This is really happening. He's going to pull out a little box, and he's going to ask me to marry him. My heart beats erratically, as if it's going to jump right out of my chest. Sweat builds in the palms of my hands. I keep telling myself to smile and remain calm.

"So, Charlie," Kaleb draws my attention back to him instead of his hand. He takes a few deep breaths. "I've been given this wonderful opportunity out in California…" He pulls an envelope out of his pocket and places it on the table.

My gaze jumps to the envelope then back to him. "What is this?"

"Well, if you let me finish. I've been given that job promotion, but they need me to relocate to California and I want you to come with me. What do you say?"

My mouth opens and then closes like a fish out of water. Just then the waitress comes by to take our order. I blurt out, "Tequila. Make it a double. Or just bring the bottle."

"And what would you like for an entrée?" the waitress asks.

"Whatever he's having." I brush her off while reaching for my wine glass just so I can have something to drink.

Kaleb orders Lobster Pappardelle for the both of us before the waitress walks away. Hopefully, to get my tequila.

"I'm sorry I caught you off guard. I didn't realize it was going to be this… intense. It's not like I was popping the question."

I take another drink. "Yeah, glad it wasn't that," I scoff.

"Charlie, you mean a lot to me, and I would love if you came with me. We can share an apartment. I'm sure you can find a job out there." Kaleb opens the envelope and shows me pictures of his new office and his apartment and this beautiful park that is right across the street.

"Look, Kaleb, you mean a lot to me too. I'm so happy to have met you and you've been amazing…"

"I feel like there's a but coming."

"But I just don't know. You sprung this on me. When are you leaving? When do I need to let you know? What am I going to do about my lease? My job? My friends?" Just thinking about everything is causing me to hyperventilate.

"You don't have to decide right this minute. But I leave in two weeks. This was an opportunity I couldn't pass up. You know how hard I've worked for this promotion."

"I know. I know. I can't ask you to stay. I just don't know if I can go."

As I stare into his chocolate eyes, I can see the sadness behind them. Like I'm breaking his heart. Our entrees arrive, and we enjoy our meal in-between awkward silence and meaningless small talk. Unsure on what to say. The unspoken words kind of say everything that needs to be said. We finish up our dinner and Kaleb drives me home. Silence fills the space around us. I peek a glance at his profile while he drives, and I can see the hurt on his face. His hands grip the steering wheel just a little harder than normal. Tension resting in his stiff shoulders. I wish I could give him what he wants but that's just not in the cards for me. The car pulls up to my apartment and I don't wait for Kaleb to come around to open my door. I exit and make my way to the front of my building. Kaleb catches up to me by the time I pull open the main door. I whirl around to halt his progress. With a weak smile I lift my head and stare into his hopeful eyes. "Kaleb… I just don't think I can."

He drops his head and nods. "I get it." Looking back up he gives me a half smile. "You are a great girl, Charlie. I'm going to be jealous of the next guy who catches your attention. Take care." Kaleb drops a kiss on my cheek before he turns and ambles back to his car.

Frozen in place, I stand on the stoop and watch one of the best guys I've ever been with disappear out of my life. I watch until his taillights disappear into the night, and I ascend the stairs to my cold and lonely apartment, but thoughts of Adonis21 come back to the forefront of my mind.

CHAPTER SEVENTEEN

This is my second chance

Bennett

"Dude, where were you this weekend?" Trey is perched in the chair in front of my desk. "We missed you at Porter's. Onyx Stone played again, and I swear they have some of the hottest groupies."

"It was pretty entertaining to watch each and every woman shoot you down too," Seth quips as he shoves Trey's shoulder. "It was hilarious when you were talking to one woman and then her boyfriend appeared."

"She was totally flirting back with me. Touching my forearm. Giggling. Then a big, burly guy tapped me on the shoulder and put his arm around the girl. Trey shrugs half-heartedly and leans back in his chair, placing his ankle on his knee.

"With the look he gave you, I'm surprised he didn't punch you in the face," Seth says.

"Me too. This face is too pretty for a broken nose." Trey motions around his face. "But if he was your size. I could've taken him." He looks over to Seth.

Seth sits up straighter, offended. "Whatever. I could take you."

"Come on, have you ever been in a fight?" Trey asks.

Seth looks down to the floor. "Well… no."

"See, my point exactly." Trey playfully nudges Seth's arm. "So anyway, this guy was older, full beard, and tattoos. I bet he was her sugar daddy or perhaps just a daddy."

Shaking my head, I bark out a laugh. "Damn, I can't believe I missed that. That kind of shit only happens to you."

With a smirk on his face, Trey shrugs as if this is just an everyday occurrence in his world.

"Mark was out of town for the weekend for work and Liana's washing machine broke and according to Liana when you have two kids you can't have a non-working washing machine." I give a half smile. I'll always be there for my sister, whatever she needs. "So, my weekend was spent at her place."

"Next time. That band killed it. They'll be playing again," Trey says. He points his thump towards Seth like a hitchhiker. "I may have struck out, but this guy got some dirty bar bathroom action. All I saw was a tall red head practically dragging him down the hallway toward the bathrooms. So, Casanova, who was the girl?"

A tinge of pink covers his cheeks as Seth adjusts his black rim glasses. "A gentleman doesn't kiss and tell."

"Bullshit," Trey blurts out. "You're no gentleman. I've heard the stories. Like that one time in college."

We all bust out laughing knowing exactly what time Trey is referring to. Seth's freshman year of college he lived in the dorms. A drunken night after finals, Seth brought home a girl and either forgot or didn't give a fuck as they climbed onto the top bunk to do some not so gentlemanly things. The kicker was his roommate was asleep in the bottom bunk and the gentle rocking did not lull him to sleep. And I'm sure the screams of "Oh, yes!" "Fuck me harder" and "Your cock is so big" didn't help either. Needless to say, Seth found himself with his own room for the rest of the semester.

"Well, either way, I'm not telling you two assholes." Seth points back and forth between us. "It was one time and a stressful semester. I'm not like you two with your random hook-ups and one-night stands."

I fake cough into my hand. "Bullshit"

Seth pushes his chair back while he stands. "You guys are assholes. I got work to do."

Trey interrupts him before he can get to the door. "Game. Tonight. Don't forget."

"Yeah. Yeah. See you guys later." Seth closes the door behind him.

Trey leans back in his chair and rests his arm on the backrest to get comfortable. "I think I know who the chick is."

Feigning interest, I sit ramrod straight in my chair and scoot to the edge while clasping my hands on the desk. "Are we gossiping now?" I quirk an eyebrow.

"Fine, I won't tell you." Trey crosses his arms over his chest and looks up to the corner of the room.

Well damn, now I'm kind of interested.

"Ok, who do you think it is?"

"No, I don't want to, as you say… gossip." Trey uses air quotes on the last word.

"Alright, it's not gossip." *Yes, it is. I just won't tell Trey that.* "Just tell me who."

Trey sits up in his chair and leans forward like he's telling a secret. "Alright so I'm at the bar with Seth because I had to find a new wingman since my old one had to fall in love and shit."

I roll my eyes at his comment

"We had a few drinks. I was busy chatting with this chick While Seth left and did his own thing. A little bit later I spotted a red head lead him down the hallway but because I pay attention to shit, I noticed a shiny, sparkly thing in her hair."

"Oh, a sparkly thing. That tells us exactly who this girl is," I say sarcastically.

"Do you want to know or not?" Trey's shoulders stiffen as his lips form a thin line.

I wave my hand in front of Trey, motioning for him to continue.

"Well, later that night, we ran into Olivia and Parisa. Parisa turned her head to talk to someone and there was a shiny, sparkly thing in her hair, calling to me like a beacon."

"So red hair and shiny, sparkly thing. Okay, Sherlock Holmes. Glad you solved that mystery." I chuckle.

Trey throws his chair back and storms to the door. As he reaches for the doorknob, he spins around. He narrows his eyes at us. "I'm going to prove it. Then we will see who has the last laugh."

"Yeah, yeah. Now get out of my office. I have way too much shit to do and not enough time." Trey exits, closing the door behind him. I tilt my head. Seth and Parisa. Those two would be an interesting couple.

My eyes feel like eighty grit sandpaper. Hours have passed and I've barely made a dent in the paperwork on my desk and my email won't stop pinging. Needing a break, I pick up the phone and dial Trey.

"Hey. Meet me in the lobby. Five minutes. I need a break."

I hang up the phone, finish up a quick email, grab my suit jacket and make my way down to the lobby. As I step off the elevator, Trey is waiting at the front desk, talking to Olivia and Charlie. I slow my pace as I eavesdrop on their conversation.

"Girl, I still can't believe he just sprung that on you. Who gives someone two weeks to decide to move halfway across the country?" Olivia asks.

"What did you tell him?" Trey leans on the desk.

Charlie looks up at him, pausing her sorting of Skittles into colored piles. "Well, what could I say? I like the guy, but that's a big move and I can't just give up everything here and move two thousand miles away. So, I had to tell him I couldn't leave."

They continue talking, but I don't hear any of it. My heartbeat flutters in my throat. Charlie is single again. I had my opportunity before, and I blew it. This is my second chance. I can't fuck it up this time.

"Hey Trey, you ready?" I call out, startling all three. Charlie's hazel eyes meet mine, and I can't help giving her my panty dropping smile because that's exactly what I want to do to her. And I top off my seductive smile with a wink. She cocks her head to the side and gives me a mystified look as a slight smile plays on her lips. With that, Trey and I are out the door.

CHAPTER EIGHTEEN

A plan to make plans

Bennett

I click the channel button, not finding anything to hold my interest. Every few seconds I glance at my phone from the corner of my eye, willing it to ding. Instead of going out with everyone else this Friday night, I'm at home like a lovesick teenager, pining over a crush. All I'm missing is a pint of Chunky Monkey and an endless supply of romantic comedies. Once I heard Charlie broke up with her boyfriend, I spent all week crafting the perfect plan. How to finally get the girl, but they all seemed too desperate. So, why not go back to where it all began? I sent her a message and now I'm waiting.

Feeling like a ball of restless energy, I stand and make my way to the garage. Perhaps some manual labor is the distraction I need. The next few hours are spent sanding a custom tabletop for a neighbor down the road. Saw dust flutters around my garage when my phone pings with a message. I wipe the sweat from my brow and glance at my phone.

Emberella55: Hey stranger! Long time no talk. How have you been?

We spent the next several hours exchanging messages. Mostly just small talk about how life's going, work, and then the holy grail of information when she tells me she broke it off with her boyfriend because he was moving. Jackpot! This is my in.

Adonis21: He's a dumbass to let such a great girl like you get away.

Emberella55: Well, he did ask me to move halfway across the country to be with him.

Adonis21: Would it be too forward of me to say that I'm glad you didn't?

Emberella55: Well, no, but why would it matter if I moved or not?

Adonis21: I like knowing you're close. That there is a chance we could meet. Maybe we already have?

Emberella55: OMG! How crazy would that be if we've actually run into each other and didn't even know. I guess I've seen your abs and I feel like I could point those out in a lineup. Maybe I'll have to ask every guy I meet to lift his shirt.

My heart rate spikes as I read that first sentence. Time to divert the conversation.

Adonis21: So, you look at my picture often? Have it memorized?

Emberella55: Spank bank, remember? *winking face emoji*

Adonis21: Well, I do have your cleavage picture saved on my wallpaper.

Emberella55: Shut up! You do not!

Adonis21: *shrugs emoji*

Emberella55: Ha! I don't know whether I should be flattered or creeped out?

Adonis21: Flattered. Definitely Flattered.

Emberella55: Well, it's getting late. I should probably get to bed. It was really great chatting with you again.

Adonis21: Wait.

Adonis21: What do you think about actually meeting in person?

Emberella55: Yeah?

Adonis21: Yeah.

Emberella55: Meet the guy who has my cleavage as his wallpaper? *thinking face emoji* Perhaps this can be arranged.

Adonis21: I just really want to see if you can pick out my abs in a lineup.

Emberella55: Challenge accepted.

Adonis21: I'll let you get your beauty sleep, and we'll talk tomorrow and make plans.

Emberella55: A plan to make plans. I like it. Good night.

Adonis21: Night.

Glancing at the clock, I see it's almost two a.m. Hours feel like minutes when I'm talking to her. Needing to get some sleep myself, I make my way back to the house and take a quick shower, washing away all the saw dust from earlier. When I lay down in bed, I stare at the ceiling for a few minutes, thinking about Charlie. This is happening, I'm going to lay all my cards on the table and pray she doesn't kill me when she realizes that I'm Adonis21.

CHAPTER NINETEEN

I can't do this

Charlie

"You guys, I'm kind of freaking out here!" After making plans with Adonis21—wait, how do I not know his real name? That just spiked my anxiety to a new level. After we made plans, we chatted for the rest of the week. Just more basic getting to know you kinda questions. I could talk with him for hours about anything and everything. He's funny and quick witted. Just thinking about him puts a cheesy grin on my face and I haven't even met him. But I feel like I've known him for years. We have been talking on and off on FLIRT for close to four months now. The relationship has definitely grown into a friendship of sorts. Perhaps a pen pal? Do people still have those?

"We're on our way. I should be there in about five minutes." Olivia's voice from the three-way call pulls me out of my daze.

"If people knew how to drive, I would be there sooner," Parisa chimes in.

"We'll be there soon. Hang tight," Olivia says.

After I hang up, my feet carry me from one side of the

room to the other. I need to rid myself of this nervous energy. I shouldn't be nervous. This guy knows me, he just hasn't actually seen me. Well, minus my cleavage.

The buzz from the intercom startles me and I make a dash for it, needing my best friends. I press the button to let them up and pace in front of my door. Every few seconds I check the peep hole and when I see them round the corner, I yank open the door. "Thank God you guys are here!"

Olivia and Parisa charge into my apartment like two women on a mission. Relief falls over me knowing they're here, and I can count on them to know exactly what to do.

"I hope you're not wearing just that to dinner?" Parisa eyes me skeptically from head to toe.

I look down and see a silk slip I'm wearing. "Uh no… but I told him I'll be wearing navy dress and I don't know which one to wear."

I collapse to the floor and throw my hands over my face like this is the most difficult decision I've had to make.

Parisa takes charge and directs Olivia to my second bedroom to get the clothing situation under control. She then helps me up off the floor, grabs my shoulders, and gives me a little shake while looking me square in the eyes. "Charlie, you are beautiful and strong, and this guy is lucky that you agreed to meet him. Don't ever forget that. Now, let's get you in there and get you into the perfect dress that he'll be dying to rip off you by the end of the night."

I give a slight nod and follow close behind her. As we enter, Olivia has a handful of dresses laid out on the ottoman for me to try on.

"I have everything from 'does this dress make me look hot' to 'I want you to rip this off with your teeth.'" Olivia motions her hand over the stack.

"I suggest we start with the latter, but first the slip has to go. No one wears those anymore," Parisa states.

Olivia grabs for the dress on top and passes it to me.

"Plus, with this dress, you kinda can't wear anything under it."

After trying on a few dresses, I settle on wearing something more in the middle of housewife and hoe. The girls finish helping me with my hair and make-up. When they're finished, I glance at myself in the full-length mirror. My hair is in a loose updo and my smokey eye makeup is on point. The deep navy off the shoulder, billowing bodice and multi sheared thigh high dress hugs my hips and ass perfectly.

"Aww Charlie, you look so beautiful. He's going to be picking his jaw up off the floor when he sees you," Parisa says.

"Well, at least then you'll know which guy he is," Olivia chimes in.

I pull up to the restaurant we agreed to meet at, thankful it's not The Boat House, and park in the lot like all the other commoners. The forty dollars it cost for valet is much better spent on groceries than parking. Plus, this will buy me a few extra minutes to settle my nerves. I've never been to this restaurant as it's a place out of my price range, but he insisted and told me he was paying. As I meander through the parking lot, I white knuckle my clutch, not because I feel unsafe, but because I am nervous as hell. But I shouldn't be nervous. I feel this guy knows me, the real me. He knows all my favorites, ranging from food, to color, to flower.

Soft yellow twinkle lights decorate the top of a large canopy that covers the walkway into the restaurant, creating a soft ambient glow. I inhale a few deep breaths before I make my way towards the front door. A doorman greets me as he holds the door open. As I stride down the long hallway to the hostess stand, I notice several small windows that peer into the dining area. I slow my steps, trying to glance inside and see if I can catch a glimpse of him. Just when I catch a glimpse of someone who could be him, my shoe catches on the lip of a rug causing me to tumble forward, arms windmilling. Luckily, I catch my balance before diving headfirst into the large wooden hostess stand. Several diners glance my way, curious about the commotion. So now, not only am I nervous but also embarrassed. This night is going well so far.

"Oh, Miss, are you alright?" The young hostess rushes to my side.

"Yeah, I'm fine, thanks." I brush down my dress to make sure nothing is out of place. "But if you see my dignity back there. Just please return it."

"Yes, ma'am." She releases a soft chuckle. "What can I help you with this evening?"

"I am meeting someone here. I was told to give you the name Mr. Adonis."

She looks down at her book and glances back at me, a smile playing on her lips. "Right this way. Please follow me."

I follow behind her as we travel under a brick archway. I quickly peer around the room, trying to guess which table we're headed to. Aromas of rosemary and fresh baked bread waft through the air. An enormous wine cellar that would make any wine enthusiast jealous sits along the wall to my right. On the left is a brick wall lined with high back booths as pennant lights fall over each table.

I'm trying to look at faces, even though I don't know what his face looks like. We are coming up to a lone two-person table in the back corner of the restaurant. The guy has his back to us, and I can see short dark hair, a little longer on the top and fades on the sides. He's dressed in a dark suit.

Time slows with each step that we get closer. My heartbeat pounds in my throat. I brush my palms on the side of my dress. This is it. This is the moment. The hostess waves her hand to finish directing me to the table and quickly scurries away to give us some privacy. As I come up to the side of the table, I see his elbows are resting on the tabletop, his hands steepled together, his head cast downward.

"Well, hello there, Mr. Adonis," I say with a sultry smile on my face.

His eyes dart up to me and my heart stops. What the fuck is happening right now? Am I being punked? I glance around to see if people start jumping out from behind fake plants and from under tables with video cameras. When I peer back down at him, it's the same guy I've worked with for just over a year. The same guy who I've seen bring countless women to his office. The same guy who was a complete asshole to me at the bar. And the same guy I once drunkenly kissed.

"What are you doing here?" I whisper yell.

He gives me a sheepish smile. Points to himself. "Adonis21. You must be Emberella55. But I preferred SexKitten69."

Blink

Blink

Blink

"I can't do this." Turning on my heel, I storm out of the restaurant. I weave in and out of the parked cars, the click of my heels on the pavement growing louder with each stomp of irritation. Right before I arrive at my car a hand grabs my elbow and whirls me around.

"Please. Let me explain." Bennett immediately drops my elbow when he me glare at him.

"Explain? Explain what?" I shriek. "Explain how you played me? How long have you known it was me? Oh, God…" I cover my face with my hands. "The pictures. You have pictures. You saw pictures."

"Let's just go sit down inside. I'll explain," Bennett pleads.

"I can't do this. It's too much."

I walk away and again he grabs me to turn me around, but

this time his lips crash to mine. Soft yet commanding. A soft whimper escapes my lips. One hand cups my cheek, the other clasps around the nape of my neck as if to never let me go. He tilts his head, wanting to deepen the kiss. But I can't. I break away from his hold and push at his chest.

"You don't get to kiss me and expect everything to be okay. It doesn't work like that. I can't trust you."

I turn on my heel and walk past my car. So much anger courses through my veins right now, I know there is no way I can drive. My hands shake as I fumble to pull my phone out of my clutch to call Olivia. I give her the code word and tell her to pick up Parisa to grab my car. I chance one last look behind me and Bennett is still standing on the sidewalk. His hands threading through his hair as he looks down at the pavement. I turn back around, unable to look at him any longer.

CHAPTER TWENTY

Go get the girl

Bennett

I'm the biggest piece of shit known to man. None of that went down the way I was expecting. *What were you expecting, dumbass?* Would she be upset? Maybe. But to completely shut me out and walk away. Wasn't expecting that. I've sent her a few messages explaining everything, how I only created a profile to appease my sister, and that I randomly stumbled upon her account. Also, that I didn't know it was her until I overheard her talking about her ex using it to cheat. But by that time, I was in too deep. I enjoyed talking to her, and I didn't want it to stop. She saw every single one of my messages but never responded.

Every day this week, I had her favorite flowers delivered to her desk with an apology note, hoping she would talk to me. And every day I would find the flowers either in the trash, left in front of my office door, and one time given to a complete stranger who walked in asking for directions. Trey was there to witness that one. With one last flower attempt, I had a bouquet of her favorite flowers and another apology note sent to her desk. As I watched from outside my second-floor office, those flowers sat on her desk all day. When she left for the weekend, she took the flowers with her. I took that as a good sign.

Sitting at the bar at Porter's, I spill all of this to their newest bartender, Rylee. She listens as if she was my therapist. Doesn't pass any judgment. Just tops off my beer when she sees my glass is almost empty. But when I finish telling her what happened, she did a one-eighty.

"God, you're such a dumbass. You gotta man up and go see this girl!" She slams her hands on the bar top.

Catching me off guard, I tilt my head to the side and look at her as if she has three heads. And maybe because of these beers she does.

"You send her flowers and a cheesy note, but come on, woo the girl." She throws her arms in the air. "What's wrong with guys these days and not knowing how to woo a girl?" Rylee mutters to herself. Ducking down to meet me at eye level. "You can't do that with just flowers. She didn't throw the last ones in the trash. That's a good sign, but don't stop there." She stands to her full height and puts one hand on her hip. "If you like this girl, go get her. Big grand gesture. Have you never watched a romantic comedy?"

I stare at her and shake my head.

She huffs before placing her hands on the bar top in front of me. "Patrick serenades Kat in front of the entire soccer team in *10 Things I Hate About You*. Lloyd held the boombox over his head in *Say Anything*. Edward got on a fire escape for Vivian in *Pretty Woman* even though he's afraid of heights. Big Grand gesture." She tosses the bar rag to rest on her shoulder. "And I have a feeling she likes you too because a girl who's not interested wouldn't react like that."

"So, what you're saying is I need to serenade her in front of a bunch of people with a boombox on a fire escape?"

"You might be a lost cause," she mumbles. "No, what I'm saying is you need to make it big and make it memorable."

I take a moment to let everything she said sink in.

Go get the girl, big grand gesture… Got it.

I throw a stack of cash on the bar and thank Rylee. I'm going to get my girl.

My Uber drops me off at her apartment but when I reach the main door, it's locked. Fuck. This isn't going as planned. I pace the front entrance trying to think of ways I could get inside when suddenly the door opens, and a younger couple strolls out. Grabbing the door handle before it can close, I offer a quick thank you and rush inside. *Shit, I don't know which one is her apartment.* "Excuse me?" I yell down to the couple who are only a few steps down the sidewalk. "Charlie Hansley lives in this building. Any chance you know which number she is?

The couple talk amongst themselves for a moment before the guy yells back. "She's right next to me. Second floor. Apartment four."

"Thanks man." I turn around and hike up the stairs two at a time. On the entire car ride over here, I silently gave myself a pep talk. I won't lose the girl this time. I'll lay it all out there and pray that she forgives me. When I reach her doorway, I come to a stop. My heart racing, partially from running up the stairs, but mostly from what her answer will be. I take a few deep breaths and quietly rap on her door.

Silence.

I knock one more time.

The echo from my knock is the only sound in the hallway. With my ear to the door, I try to listen for any sign of movement on the other side. A few beats pass and nothing. I rest my hands on the door jamb and lower my head. Defeated.

Suddenly, the click of a dead bolt unlatching jolts me back to life. I watch as the door handle turns, and the door opens a crack.

"Bennett? Is that you? What are you doing here?" Charlie asks softly. Her hair's slightly disheveled, and a robe wraps around her small frame.

"Charlie. Look. Please hear me out. Can I come in?"

My heart rate speeds up, waiting for her response. When her eyes connect with mine, I sense wariness as she seems reluctant but opens the door, anyway. I let out a small sigh of relief and she motions for me to enter. She closes the door softly behind her and folds her arms over her chest.

"Okay. You're here. What do you have to say that you haven't said already?"

I rake my hands through my hair and then look up at Charlie.

"I'm an asshole."

She folds her arms over her chest. "You deceived me for months. I sent you pictures of myself. Did anyone else see those?"

I move my head from side to side. "Trey tried, but I stopped him before he could get to my phone."

"So, everyone knew but me." She releases a humorless laugh as her arms fall to her sides. "Was it all a big joke? Let's catfish the girl who was cheated on."

"Fuck. Charlie. It was never like that. I should've told you who I was as soon as I found out who you were, but…" I turn around and start pacing around the small area. My eyes catch sight of my flowers sitting on her small two-person dining table. "Rylee told me I need some big grand gesture to win you back. But I don't have a boombox. I can't sing worth shit." I glance around the room. "I'm not sure if you have a fire escape or not. But I've enjoyed talking to you. It felt real. And I didn't want that to end. Call me selfish, but I didn't mean to hurt you." In a few strides I'm standing directly in front of her. "So, I'm here as a man who can't stop thinking about this amazing woman and will do whatever it takes for her to forgive me. Please forgive me. If you never want to talk to me again, fine. But just please forgive me?" She ponders my plea for a few moments while my words sink in and in that moment, I've never felt so vulnerable. My chest tightens with each passing second, she doesn't say anything. So, I offer her one last piece of me. "I was never the guy who chased the girl but here I am because you mean so damn much to me. I'm so sorry."

After what feels like an eternity her face slowly lifts to mine. "I've enjoyed talking to you, too," she says in the faintest of whispers.

"Yeah?" A smile tugs at my lips.

She bites her bottom lip and nods.

"So, you forgive me?" I take another step closer until my shoes are touching her bare toes.

With her eyes still locked on mine, she nods.

"And you want to see where this might go?"

She nods again, but this time lust blazes behind her orbs. "But you need to make it up to me."

With her body pressed between mine and the door. I stare down into her hazel eyes, flecks of gold circle her pupils as I search for any hint that she doesn't want this. I bend down and tilt my head to the side, my cheek touching hers, and whisper.

"I will spend eternity making it up to you. But the next move is yours."

Her hands rise to rest on my forearms. When I glance at her face, her eyes are closed, but slowly they open, and I see a spark of heat and desire pool in her irises. Ever so slowly, her hands glide up past my biceps until her fingers are clasped behind my neck. Time stands still as I wait with bated breath on what she is going to do. She stretches up on her tippy toes and places the softest of kisses on my lips. She starts to pull away when I wrap my arms around her waist and pull her to me. Her robe falls open as her body presses against mine. I crash my lips to hers and a moan escapes her throat. She tilts her head and I deepen the kiss. Hard and punishing. Her lips part as an invitation I gladly take. The kiss continues as my hands roam to her round, plump ass. I give it a squeeze and am greeted with another moan. I wrap my hands behind her thighs and lift her, pressing her up against the door. Her hands thread through my hair as my growing erection presses against her core.

I can't get enough of this girl.

She starts to grind on my cock through my jeans and I press harder into her. I pepper kisses down her cheek, then to the nape of her neck. I pull the robe off her shoulder and kiss her collarbone. All the while, her hands roam my back, then her fingers glide through my hair. Little whimpers and moans escape her mouth.

"I need you so bad right now." My words are breathy as I kiss the top of her cleavage.

"Yes, I need you, too."

She moans and then leans back and starts unbuttoning my shirt. I can't help but look at her gorgeous face and then she notices me.

"What?"

"You're so damn sexy."

"Well, it's not going to be so sexy if you don't help me get this shirt off you."

She pulls and tugs to get it loose from where her legs are wrapped around me. I let out a small laugh. Her hands caress my bare chest before she runs them past my shoulders to push the shirt off.

"You got this. You don't need my help."

She glares at me and then playfully smacks my chest. "Put me down."

I slowly drop her legs and her body slides down mine.

And that's when I see what she's wearing under her robe. A silk camisole that does nothing to hide her perky tits and hard nipples and matching silk shorts that I will happily remove with my teeth.

She grabs my hand and drags me behind her, happy to follow her wherever she goes. We enter her bedroom, and the warm glow of a lamp illuminates the room. She turns around and directs me to the end of the bed.

"The abs that I've dreamed about." She finishes taking my shirt all the way off and pushes me so my back hits the bed. Charlie shrugs her robe off, and I watch as it floats to the floor. She climbs up on top of me, straddling my hips. Once again, my cock is right at her entrance. If we didn't have two layers of clothes between us, I could slip right in. She grabs my face and kisses me. We grind against each other like two teenagers until I decide it's my turn to take control.

Catching her by surprise, I flip her over in one swift motion and she lets out a soft squeal. "It's my turn to play."

I kiss her swollen, pouty lips, then I pepper kisses down her neck. She tilts her head to give me better access, her throaty moans encouraging me to continue. So, I kiss down to her collarbone and down her clothed chest. I suck on her hard nipple through the silk as my hand goes up to squeeze the other breast. Her back arches off the bed as she writhes beneath me. I slowly lift the hem of her shirt, exposing her taut stomach. Starting between her breasts, I pepper kisses down to her belly button. When I look up, she's risen to her elbows to watch me. The corner of my lips tip up into a smile. My cock twitches knowing she wants to watch what I'm about to do to her. Before I get side-tracked, I continue my exploration to the waistband of her sleep shorts. With my teeth, I grab the elastic and pull down.

"That has to be one of the hottest things I've seen," she whispers and bites her lip.

She lifts her butt off the bed, and I pull the shorts the rest of the way off with the assistance of my hands and drop them to the floor. Starting at her ankle, I place kisses on her leg, over her calf, past her knee until I get to her thigh. And then I do it all over again on the other leg.

"Bennett?"

I stop my slow, sensual seduction and look up at Charlie.

"Let me just say I love this sweet foreplay thing we're doing. But foreplay is over. I need you. Now."

A laugh escapes my lips as I place one last kiss on her thigh. I shift myself between her open legs and place a kiss on her neatly trimmed pussy. A moan escapes Charlie's mouth and I kiss her again. This time I use my fingers and spread her open and lick.

"You are so wet for me." I take another lick.

"God, yes." Charlie moans while her fingers fist the blanket.

I lap at her arousal, and her body squirms beneath me. I move one hand to her stomach to prevent her from moving while the other rubs her clit. *Rub. Lick. Rub. Lick.*

Breathy moans escape Charlie's lips. "Don't stop. I'm going to come."

I insert a finger, fucking her while I suck on her clit. My tongue continues to lick her entrance. Charlie's moans slowly subside as she comes down from her orgasm. I make my way up her body as she grabs my cheeks, bringing my lips to hers, not caring about her own taste on my lips.

She reaches down, grabbing my hard dick in my jeans. I let out a deep groan. She breaks away from the kiss to unbutton my jeans and pull them down over my hips. I make quick work to toe off my shoes. When they hit the floor, my pants soon follow. She grabs her camisole and pulls it over her head. My gaze lingers on her newly exposed skin, admiring her plump tits and erect nipples. I'll appreciate them more with my mouth later. Right now, I am dying to be inside this woman. I pull my black boxer briefs down and my hard cock springs out. Her eyes go wide as saucers as she stares at me.

"Don't worry, sweetheart. It'll fit." I give her a playful wink.

"Oh, I'm not concerned about that. I'm wondering how long or how many times I will get to enjoy that tonight."

I bark out a laugh, and she smiles up at me. I tackle her to the bed. She spreads her legs and I nestle between them.

"Well, let's find out, shall we?"

Her wet pussy rubs against my aching cock. In one quick motion I could press into her, but she reaches over to open the drawer on the nightstand and pulls out a pack of condoms. I grab one from her, tearing open the foil, pulling out the condom, and sliding it over my cock. I place my lips on hers as I slowly push into her.

She breaks away from our kiss and moans. I rock my hips back and forth, picking up momentum with each thrust. Soon she is lifting her hips to meet me with every pump.

I dip my head to kiss her breast.

"You feel so good," I say as I swirl my tongue around her nipple. "Your pussy is so tight. It's milking my cock."

Thrust.

Thrust.

Thrust.

I feel my balls tighten up as her pussy contracts, gripping my dick. We both moan out in ecstasy as our orgasms hit at the same time. We slow our movements and rise, resting my weight on my elbows, and look down. Her hair is fanned out over her pillow, and she has a sedated look behind her hooded eyes, but she's never looked more beautiful. I give her a kiss because I don't think I will ever tire of kissing this girl.

"Where's your bathroom? I'll get this cleaned up".

She points to a half-closed door just outside her bedroom. I get up and dispose of the condom and bring a wet washcloth to clean Charlie. Afterwards, she lifts the blanket and invites me back in. I can't say I'm one to snuggle after sex, but right now I'll give this girl anything she wants.

"I just want a couple of minutes. None of this after sex talk. Just a couple minutes." Charlie snuggles into my chest, and I wrap my arm around her. A few moments later, I can hear her soft breaths as she sleeps.

CHAPTER TWENTY-ONE

I don't want to think of you with anyone else

Charlie

Light shines through the half open curtain, causing me to roll over. I open one eye to glance at the alarm clock and instead of seeing the time, I see a man's black button-down shirt. Just then, everything from last night comes crashing into me like a ton of bricks.

Bennett.

Pressed against the door.

The kissing.

Ripping off each other's clothes.

The sex. Mind you, amazing sex. But still sex.

I shoot up out of bed, my eyes frantically scanning the room for any other sign of Bennett. My comforter drops to my lap. A blast of cold hits me and I realize I'm still naked. Bennett must be around here somewhere. He wouldn't be that desperate to escape. He wouldn't leave his shirt, would he? *That jerk left!*

I search the room for my robe and then the clank of pans coming from the kitchen gets my attention. Throwing on my robe, I walk out to the kitchen and holy shit. A girl could get used to that sight.

Bennett is standing at my stove. Barefoot. His jeans riding low on his hips. His dark hair wild as if someone was tugging on it all night. *Wait, I was.* Then there's the way his back muscles flex as he whisks at whatever's in the bowl in front of him. I lean against the doorjamb, admiring the view until I'm caught.

"See something you like?" The corners of Bennett's lips upturn slightly.

"Well, actually I do." I push off the door and saunter my way into the kitchen.

"This smells delicious." I take a whiff of whatever he's cooking.

When I'm standing next to him, he turns towards me, lightly grips my biceps and pushes me until my butt hits the counter. Dipping down he places a chaste kiss on my lips, the taste of freshly brewed coffee still lingering on his, and then he continues cooking.

"You didn't have much to work with in your fridge. But I have some bacon and eggs. Coffee's made." He reaches over to my indoor herb garden to pluck some parsley out of the DIY mason jar plant holder hanging from the wood plank on the wall.

"You know you're not supposed to cook bacon without a shirt on?"

"Why?" Just then, the bacon splatters and gets him right in the chest. Bennett jumps back from the offending bacon.

"That's why." I chuckle and move to sit at the kitchen island after grabbing a cup of coffee. "Move in with me. Just so I can have this every day." I take a sip.

Bennett shakes his head, and his shoulders shake from laughter. He sets two plates of food in front of us and takes a seat next to me. We both dig in and start eating. A moan escapes when the first bite hits my tongue.

"Well, that's a sound I remember from last night." A sly smile plays on his lips.

"Shut up!" I smack his arm. I bow my head to hide my flushed cheeks.

"I won't lie. It's a sound I hope to hear more often."

I drop my fork and turn to him.

"Okay, serious talk. What are we doing?"

Bennett rotates towards me and clasps my hands in his. "Well, we are going to finish breakfast. Then we are going to go back to that room and do more of what we did last night."

"As amazing as that sounds. I mean, what are *we* doing?" I ask as I point between the two of us. "Are we dating? Just sex? One-time thing."

"Look Charlie, I like you. I like you a lot. I've liked you since way before you drunkenly kissed me outside Porter's."

Whoa this is news to me.

"I want this to be more than sex and I definitely want this to be more than one time." He grabs my chin and places a kiss on my lips. He looks directly into my eyes. "Now, what does that make us?"

"Dating?" I ask hesitantly.

"Dating. Exclusively. I don't want to think of you with anyone else."

"I like the sound of that."

I get off my chair and move between his legs and give him a kiss. His hand comes up to rest on my hips and I deepen the kiss. I break away from Bennett and saunter my way back to the bedroom. Looking over my shoulder, I see Bennett watching my every move. I untie my robe and let it flutter to my feet. Bennett gets up from his stool and chases after me. Breakfast now forgotten.

CHAPTER TWENTY-TWO

I want to see your wood

Bennett

It was hard leaving her all alone in bed. I wanted to stay cuddled up to her, inhaling her sweet, jasmine scent but my sister and her husband were on their way over to drop off a load of wood. The missed phone calls and ignored messages tells me I will have some explaining to do when I see her.

Just as I turn off the shower, I hear their truck pull into my driveway. I throw on some clothes and meet them outside.

"Hey, guys! Thank you so much for this." I wrap my arms around Liana in a tight hug and hold out my hand for Mark to shake. "Holy shit, what am I going to do with all this?" I walk around Mark's tandem axel car trailer, stacked full of old barn wood. A friend of theirs was tearing down an old barn, and they thought all this would be perfect for me to repurpose since everyone wants reclaimed barn wood furniture and decor. Just looking at the pile, I know I could make a pretty penny on all this. And I see no issue finding buyers for everything.

"I don't know, but whatever you do with it, I get first pick.

But more importantly, where were you this morning?" Liana asks with her hand on her hip and eyebrow raised.

"What's it to you?" I give her a cocky grin.

"I knew it! I know that look! You were with a girl." Liana points her finger at me and spins to her husband. "You owe me twenty bucks."

"I call bullshit. You don't know that based on a look," Mark says.

"I've known this guy for thirty-four years. Believe me. I know that look," Liana rebuts.

"There's no way you can tell by a look." They then start arguing amongst themselves.

"Hey! Hey! You guys! I'm standing right here," I say but they're not paying attention.

I go into the garage and grab a couple of beers and a bottle of water. When I come back out, they are still arguing, and I decide to break the bad news to Mark that he's about to lose twenty dollars.

"I was with a girl. In fact, I was with Charlie." I take a swig of my beer. Both of them stop talking and turn to me with a what the hell expression on their faces. I pass them their drinks and take another drink of mine. Finally, recognition crosses Liana's face.

"Wait, the same Charlie from months ago? The one you were obsessing over?" Liana questions.

"I wasn't obsessing."

"You were totally obsessing."

I glance at Mark, hoping he takes my side, but he nods in agreement.

"But also… Charlie!" Liana squeals. "Tell us everything! What happened? Tell us everything!"

"Well, maybe not everything," Mark replies.

"Also, I told you so! You owe me." Liana turns to Mark with her hand held out, waiting to collect her winnings.

I give them the cliff notes of everything that happened

from the restaurant, the groveling, and then the reunion, but leaving out the intimate details.

"Awww, my baby brother is in love." Liana's eyes light up. "When do we get to meet her? Bring her over for Sunday dinner!"

My eyes go wide and my heart thunders in my throat at Liana's comment. "Love. I don't know about that. But I'll see about dinner."

We spent the rest of the afternoon removing all the wood from the trailer and placing it in my workshop. After Liana and Mark leave, I make a mental note of what I have, along with what potential projects I could build. Pulling out a stool, I take off my shirt to wipe the sweat before it drips down my face. Spending all afternoon talking with my sister and Mark about Charlie solidifies my feelings for her. I'm done looking. The FLIRT app is useless to me now. She is everything that I want. I pull out my phone to delete the app just as my phone buzzes. Charlie's name fills the screen, and I can't help the smile as I answer.

"Hey, beautiful."

"Hey yourself. What are you up to?"

"Oh, just staring at my wood."

"I don't know whether to leave you to your moment or be jealous I'm not there."

A deep laugh escapes my chest. "Well, you are welcome to stare at my wood any time you like. Just say the word. But this time it's actual wood. Some old barn wood my sister and her husband, Mark, dropped off. I'm just trying to decide what I want to build."

"Wait, you're a carpenter too? How did I not know this? What do you make?"

"Tables, chairs, décor pieces. Sometimes I'll do custom pieces. Whatever I can restore or repurpose."

"That's amazing. I want to see."

"Well, come over. I'd be happy to show you what my

hands can do. If you catch my drift." I rattle off my address to her.

"You're insatiable." She lets out a laugh. "I'll be over soon."

Thirty minutes later, Charlie's white Chevy Trailblazer pulls into my driveway, and I can't keep the smile off my face. As soon as she puts the SUV in park, I'm opening her door, unable to wait another minute to see her. She takes my hand and steps out. Her yellow sundress flutters in the unseasonably warm breeze while I take a second to admire her beauty.

"Oh, a girl could get used to this kind of greeting," Charlie says as her eyes sweep over my bare chest.

"I wanted to make sure you'd be able to find the place. Since you can spot my abs in a lineup and all."

A blush creeps up Charlie's cheeks as she hides her face in my chest. "You're never going to let me live that down, are you?"

"Nope."

"Before I find a hole to crawl in and die, why don't you show me around. I want to see what your hands can do." She winks at me and tugs me towards the open garage.

"If you want to see what my hands can do, we're headed in the wrong direction. The house is over there." I point in the opposite direction.

"Haha. I want to see the wood." She continues to tug on my hand.

"Again, the house is over there."

She abruptly stops, whirls around causing her dress to float around her, and narrows her eyes at me. And I can't help but laugh.

I take her into my garage and show her a few things I'm working on and describe a few things I want to build. She walks around the now filled garage, dragging her finger across some of the finished boards. I could get used to seeing her in my space.

"Where did you learn how to do all this?" Charlie picks up a piece of wood and inspects it.

I fold my arms across my chest as I lean back against my workbench. "I guess it started in high school shop class. We had to build a wooden box with a stained-glass top and a working wooden clock. From there I was fascinated by taking this ordinary piece of wood and turning it into something beautiful."

"So, what is this going to be?" She stops in front of an unfinished pile of wood.

I push off and move to stand next to Charlie. "This one will actually be for myself. It'll be a truss beam table." I show her a diagram of the finished product. "The next step is to lightly sand all the pieces before staining. I've decided on a natural stain to make the grain in the walnut pop without hiding its beauty."

Charlie looks in awe at the unfinished wood, then back up to me. "Can I help?"

"Sure. If you want." Her eyes gleam with delight at my response. How can I say no to that look? I set one table leg on top of a couple sawhorses. "I've already done a rough sanding so we will give it a light sand with one-hundred twenty grit sandpaper to clean it up." I clamp the sandpaper into the sanding block and pass it to Charlie. She holds it in her palm like a baby kitten, like she's afraid to startle it. "It won't bite." I give her a teasing smirk.

"I know. But I don't know what to do."

I reach for the sanding block and glide it across the board. After I'm done with my demonstration, Charlie takes over, moving the sanding block all over. Her tongue peeks out from the corner of her mouth as she concentrates. Before she can do any damage, I stop her.

"Here like this." I grab her hand and place it on top of the sanding block. I cover her hand with mine as I stand behind her and slowly move the block up and down the board. "You need nice long, even strokes going with the grain."

"You must get lots of practice with long and even strokes." She tosses me a flirty smile.

"You have no idea." My grip on her hand tightens as we continue sanding. My front is pressed up against her back. With each long stroke, her ass rubs against my aching dick. After the last stroke, she gives her ass a wiggle, and I know she's fucking with me. Well, two can play this game. Releasing the block, I steady my hands on the wooden table leg we're sanding, caging her in. I bow my head and whisper against the shell of her ear. "I know what you're trying to do."

Charlie rotates around in my arms, a sparkle in her hazel eyes when she rises to her tippy toes and places a soft kiss on my lips. Before I deepen the kiss, she's ducking under my arm to continue browsing around my garage.

"These are amazing." She turns to me. "You're amazing."

Within a few quick strides, I'm standing in front of her. I place my hands on her hips and lift her onto my tool bench and wedge myself between her legs.

"No, you're amazing."

"You make all these gorgeous pieces of furniture. By hand." She gestures to the table next to us. "All I can make is apparently knitted penis potholders." She releases a playful laugh.

"I beg to differ. I notice how every Friday when you bring in pastries you always make sure to get Gary a blueberry scone. And also, when you leave the bakery, you always give the homeless man who hangs out at the corner a sandwich and hot chocolate."

"How do you know about all those things?"

"Charlie, when it comes to you, I know everything."

"Stalker much."

"Not in a 'stare in your window while you sleep' kind of way."

"Good to know." She stretches up and presses her lips to mine. "But if you did, I would be sure to leave my curtains open," she whispers against my lips.

"Is that so?" I skate my hands up her thighs, taking the hem of her dress with. I place a kiss just below her ear, and she tilts her head to give me better access. Her jasmine scent mixed with the walnut sawdust is a smell I never want to forget. I'm chalking that up as my new favorite scent.

"Mmmhmmm"

She scoots closer to the edge of the bench and starts grinding herself against my hard cock.

I let out a strained groan as she continues to move against me. Her arms wrap around my neck while I continue my kissing assault down the column of her throat and to her collarbone. My hands travel around her waist and up her back until I reach the knot of her halter dress. I find the strings and tug them free. Her dress falls to her waist, exposing her plump breasts. Her hard nipples beg for attention, so I lower my head, taking a hard peak into my mouth. Sucking hard and then giving her a soft bite. Her moans fills the space, encouraging me to continue. I touch the front of her panties and rub her clit.

"You're so wet for me. Your panties are soaked."

"Yes. So wet. Just for you." She pants and arches her back, pressing her breast further in my mouth.

Pushing her panties to the side, I slide a finger into her wet pussy. Pumping in and out before adding a second finger, soon she starts riding my hand. Moving her hips back and forth while picking up speed. Removing my fingers, I slide them downward until they graze across her puckered hole. I hear a sharp intake of breath as Charlie's eyes flutter closed.

"Has anyone fucked you here?" I whisper as I add more pressure against her back entrance.

Charlie's cheeks flush as she shakes her head back and forth.

"But I recall some toys you recently bought. We might have to get those out to play."

Another moan escapes her swollen lips as I apply a little more pressure.

"Say the words, Charlie. I need words."

"Yes. Toys. We'll try the toys." She whimpers when I pull away. My fingers move back to rubbing her clit in lazy circles before plunging back into her. After a few pumps, I add a third, stretching her tight pussy. Her moans and pants fill my garage as she rides my fingers to ecstasy. Her movements slow as her orgasm subsides.

Without a second thought, I remove my hand from between her legs and drag a finger across her lips, painting them with her wetness. I lean down and kiss her glistening lips. When I pull away and look down, her tongue darts out to lick away the rest.

"Fuck. That was hot." I reach down and adjust my cock that's trying to burst from my zipper.

A car horn blares as it drives by and pulls me from my lust fill hazed. Then I remember we were in my dirty garage with the door wide open where anyone could stop in and see.

"I am far from done with you." I reach down, cupping her face. "But I would rather finish this inside, where there is no chance of prying eyes."

Before leaving, I tie up her dress, pick her up, and throw her over my shoulder. She lets out a giggle as I wrap one arm around the back of her thighs and the other around her ass as I make quick work to get her to my bedroom.

We lie in bed feeling sedated after another round of orgasms for Charlie and some of the hottest sex I've ever had. Charlie has the sheet wrapped around her body while she rests her head on my chest.

"Why did we wait so long to do this?" Charlie asks as she runs her fingertips over my chest and through the small patch of hair.

"Hook up? At first you were always off limits and the one time I tried to tell you how I felt you shot that down faster than a popped balloon."

"When you asked me to your office?" Charlie sits up. "You've liked me since then?"

"If you want to know how long I've liked you… I would say that would be the very first day when I saw you sitting behind the desk at The Blue Stone Group. You looked up at me and you had the most beautiful smile that just lit up your face. From that day, I couldn't stop thinking about you."

"But you were such a jerk! Always parading around the front desk with women hanging all over you. Doing who knows what with them in your office. You wouldn't even call me the right name."

Sitting up to lean against the headboard, I grab Charlie to tuck her into my side.

"First, those women meant nothing. They had money to spend, and I was there to help them spend it. Maybe I flirted a little, but trust me, nothing happened." I pick up her hand and bring her knuckles to my lips. "Second, I'm sorry I was a jerk. I wanted you and couldn't have you. I thought if you hated me, then it would be easier to get over you." I bring my forehead to hers and stare into her eyes. "But that didn't work."

"I'm kind of glad it didn't work. I'm learning to like you." Charlie gives me a smile.

"Well, hold that thought." I hold up a finger. "My sister wanted me to invite you over for Sunday dinner. Don't feel obligated. Think about it. I know meeting the family can be a big thing and dinner is really casual…"

"Wait, your sister knows about me? We just started dating?" Charlie interrupts.

"So, you know how I met you on FLIRT?" Charlie nods her head. "It was my sister's idea that I sign up. My mom and sister have been on my case about finding a girl and settling down, so I joined to get my sister off my back. But then I saw your picture and there was something about it that intrigued me, so I had to say something."

"Wait, you were using a fake picture. How did you know mine wasn't fake?" Her brow rises.

"I guess I didn't. I was just hoping you weren't some creepy old man, sitting in his basement with Cheeto stained fingers."

Just then, her stomach growls, interrupting our talk. Her eyes go wide, and she grabs her stomach.

"Guess I was in too much of a rush to see you. I forgot to eat."

"Let me feed you. I don't have much, but I'm sure I can find something."

"Okay. Maybe I can get a proper tour of your house. The upside-down view while you carried me to your room just didn't cut it." Charlie gives me a saucy smile while she pulls her dress up and ties it.

Once we're dressed, I lead her down to my open kitchen. While I dig through the fridge, she makes her way around my living room, looking at various furniture pieces I've made. She takes her time as she makes her way from one side of the room to the other. Familiarizing herself with the space. And damn, I can picture her here with me cuddled together on the couch with the wood-burning fireplace casting an amber glow around the room while we just talk. Because I could spend hours talking to this girl about anything and everything.

Then it hits me, I have it bad for this girl. I ponder that for a few moments, a smile tugging at my lips before I turn around and continue making a couple of sandwiches for us.

"Apparently, you have a thing for toy cars." Charlie rolls one of the toy cars on the shelf before picking it up for a closer inspection.

Rounding the kitchen island, I walk to stand next to her. "These aren't just toy cars. They're Hot Wheels and growing up I got at least one every year for my birthday. And this red one is a Porsche 930." Charlie places it back on the shelf before checking out the others. "But when I got older, I would search the internet for ones I didn't have to add to my collection. One day, I hope to pass them all along to my kids." At the mention of kids, a soft smile forms on her lips.

"Wow, you must have close to one hundred or so." Charlie looks back at me, her eyes lit up with amazement.

"Follow me." I take her hand in mine and lead her down a short hallway to another room. A warm glow fills the room when I flick the switch. Along the back wall is a row of bookshelves filled with more toy cars.

"Well, I stand corrected." Charlie laughs. Then she starts inspecting the different shelves until she stops at a glass case. "What are these ones in the case?"

"These are some rare ones I've found. Like this one." I point to a purple car. "This is a 1974 Magenta Rodger Dodger with white interior. As of today, it's worth about three thousand dollars." Charlie's eyes go wide as a full moon at the mention of the dollar amount.

"That's crazy. Who knew a little metal toy could be worth so much?" She continues her stroll around the room when she stops at my desk. "No way! Is that…"

Charlie's outburst causes me to look in her direction.

"I think I know that guy." Charlie holds up the picture, pointing to the guy wearing a shirt with Greek letters sprawled on the front.

"Mike Keller. You know Mike?" Within a few steps I'm standing next to her.

"Yes. A girl I went to high school with dated him. He was in a frat at Harbor Highlands College. She invited me out to one of their parties." She pauses for a moment, her brows wrinkle as if she's trying to remember something, then recognition registers on her face. "It was a 90s themed party. Everyone dressed up in 90s clothes and they played 90s music. Amber and I dressed up as Cher and Dee from *Clueless*." She lets out a laugh.

Suddenly, moments from that party flash through my memory like an old View-Master reel. Beer, so much beer. And then someone held up a playing card and mentioned suck and blow. I had no idea what was happening, but then a girl with the most hypnotic hazel eyes and a blonde wig, wearing a yellow plaid skirt, a white shirt that was hugging her tits, and white knee-high stockings sat next to me, and I wasn't going anywhere.

"How much do you remember from that night?" I ask.

"Uh, well, I remember I'll never eat the fruit out of a wopatui again. Me and the bushes became way more acquainted than I would have liked. I don't know why anyone would think it's a good idea to fill a cooler full of Everclear, fruit punch, and fruit."

"Is that all you remember? A blue polyester suit doesn't come to mind?"

"No…" A few beats pass and then her eyes go wide.

"Because believe it or not, my sweet Charlie, we've kissed before. And if my memory serves me right, there was a pretty good make out session in one of the upstairs bedrooms." I wink.

A blush creeps up Charlie's cheeks before she can hide her face in her hands.

"You were Harry!" she blurts out. And then falls into a fit

of laughter. "What a small world. Who knew that we had our first kiss twelve years ago?"

"And look at us now." I grab her and pull her into my arms.

"Like it was destiny." Her bright eyes look up at me.

"It's something." I lean down and place a soft kiss on her lips. "Now let's eat. You'll need some energy for what I have in store for you afterwards."

CHAPTER TWENTY-THREE

I welcome this kind of interruption

Charlie

"Charlie? Hello? Charlie?" Olivia's hands are waving through the air while she sits on the desk, her eyebrows raised.

"Huh?" I jerk my head to look at her.

"Hey, there you are! If your eyes weren't open, I'd probably think you were dead. What has you so spacey?"

"Bennett invited me over for dinner. Not like me and him dinner, like his entire family dinner."

"Oh. So, what are you going to do?" Olivia crosses her leg over the other.

"It seems like a big step." I spent the entire weekend with Bennett. In his bed, on his couch, on the table. I don't know if there is a spot in that house we haven't fooled around in or on. But it was more than that, we spent the weekend getting to know each other. My favorite part was helping him with his woodworking projects. Nothing is sexier than a tan, shirtless man swinging a hammer. Afterward, when I went back to my house, I instantly missed him.

Tapping her nails on the desk, Olivia stares at me, waiting for my answer.

"Of course, I'm going to tell him yes," I blurt out.

"Ahhh, I'm so excited for you!" Olivia claps her hands. "Who knew our Charlie would fall for the office playboy?"

"I'm going to go up and let him know." Just as I stand from my chair Parisa strolls up to the desk.

"Well, you're glowing today. But you have a leaf in your hair." Olivia reaches over to pluck the green vegetation from Parisa's locks. "And you missed a button on your blouse."

Parisa looks down and her cheeks redden when she realizes her shirt is askew. She grabs her jacket and pulls it tight around her before crossing her arms. "I was in a rush this morning. I must have missed a button. So how are you guys?"

"Did you know our girl Charlie here is going to meet the parents," Olivia says

"Well, it's not just the parents but his whole family. They do this Sunday dinner where they all get together. So yeah, it's his parents, his sister, her husband, aunts, and uncles. Oh my god, I think I might puke." My hand instinctively covers my stomach.

"You got this. Everyone will love you. Just don't bring them any of your crafting projects." Parisa gives me a playful smile while I narrow my eyes at her. "Seriously, Charlie. You have nothing to worry about."

A moment later Seth strides through the door. I watch as Parisa gives him a hard glare then abruptly turns away, but Seth's eyes are on her the entire time as he walks past. Once the sound from the elevator dings and we know Seth is gone, Parisa's shoulders fall in relief. "Well, I'm going to get this taken care of." Parisa points to her shirt. "I'll talk to you guys later." She scurries away before either me or Olivia can ask her what that was all about.

Turning toward Olivia, I ask, "Is it just me or was that weird?"

"That was most definitely weird."

I make a mental note to ask Parisa about that later but first back to the task at hand. I smooth down the imaginary wrinkles from my dress skirt before I stride over to the elevator and press the button to the second floor. It's been so long since I've done the whole meet the parents thing, I forgot how nerve wracking it can be. But Bennett wants this, wants me involved in this part of his life, and that thought puts a smile on my face.

When the elevator doors open, I make my way to Bennett's closed office door. I inhale a few deep breaths to calm my nerves before I softly knock, then I let myself in. Bennett is sitting behind his desk, a phone cord draped across his desk and a voice on the other end of the phone can be heard in the small space. I mouth *I'll come back later*, but Bennett holds up a finger and then waves me in. I turn and softly close the door. He holds his hand over the receiver and whispers he'll just be a minute.

I stride across the room, Bennett's ardent gaze watching my every movement. I trail my finger across the oversized mahogany executive desk and take a seat on the desktop, right next to him, and cross one leg over the other, the hem of my skirt riding up an inch. His gaze starts at my ankles and drifts up my leg just to where the fabric stops at my thigh.

"Rick, I have an important meeting that just came up. I'll call you back later." Before giving Rick a chance to say anything back, Bennett's hanging up the receiver. Rolling his chair over to position himself in front of me, his arms wrap around my waist, and he nuzzles my legs.

"A man could get used to this every morning in his office." He kisses the outside of my thigh.

"I hope I wasn't interrupting anything important."

"No. I welcome this kind of interruption any time."

I reach down, his five o'clock shadow tickling my fingertips, and I tilt his face towards mine.

"Well, I wanted to let you know, I would love to attend Sunday dinner with you."

"Really?"

My lips tug into a smile and I nod.

Bennett stands with both hands on either side of me and places an innocent kiss on my lips. I grab his face and deepen the kiss. My teeth tug on his bottom lip as he lets out a deep groan.

"You know, I've always had this fantasy…" My words are a faint brush across his lips.

"Oh yeah? What's that?" His breath tickles the shell of my ear.

I shove at his chest, forcing him to sit. With my hands on the armrest, I push his chair back and kneel in front of him. I place my hands on his knees and spread them. At first Bennett eyes me skeptically until realization hits, then a grin spreads across his lips as he leans back in his chair. My hands slowly dance their way up his thighs until I reach his silver belt buckle. I make quick work to unlatch the buckle and unbutton his dress pants. Peering up at him through my eyelashes, his hooded eyes stare back at me.

My fingers grip the zipper and tug down, exposing his black boxer briefs. The bulge in the fabric becoming more prominent as I peel back his pants. I take a few minutes to stroke his hardening cock through the fabric.

"Oh fuck, that feels so good." Bennett moans.

He grinds against my hand to create more friction, spurring me on more. My fingers reach for the waistband tugging down. His thick cock springs free, a bead of pre-cum leaking from the tip. Wrapping my hand around his girth, my tongue darts out to swirl around his tip, the saltiness hitting my taste buds. Bennett lifts his hips to tug down his pants giving me better access. I run my tongue along the underside, tracing his thick vein. When I reach the top, I wrap my lips around the head and suck. My hand grips his shaft moving in tandem with my mouth. With each downward stroke, I take him a little deeper.

"Charlie… fuck… keep going. You look so goddamn beautiful with my cock in your mouth." Bennett's words encourage me to continue.

Strong fingers thread through my hair, holding me in place as he gently thrusts upward as I take him deeper. The head of his cock hits the back of my throat. The intrusion causing me to swallow around his head.

"Fuuuuuck. I'm going to come."

My moan sends vibrations all around his dick as I continue stroking and sucking. A moment later, a burst of his hot seed is spilling into the back of my throat as I swallow him down. His cock twitches as he finishes his release. I free him from my mouth and glance up at him with a wide smile on my face.

His hand cups my cheek as his thumb gently brushes back and forth across the skin. "That was probably the best blow job I've ever gotten. I think every Monday morning should start off like that."

There's a knock on the door, my smile falls, and I instantly freeze.

CHAPTER TWENTY-FOUR

What are you doing down there?

Bennett

My hands fumble as I frantically tuck myself back into my pants, not bothering with my belt. I motion for Charlie to hide under the desk. She crawls under and I scoot my chair in just as I hear the click of the door right before it opens.

My head pops up as I try to keep my face as expressionless as possible.

"Hey man, gotta question…" Trey says as he enters but halts in his tracks when he sees my face. Charlie's nails dig into my leg, and I try not to flinch.

"What's going on in here?" His eyebrow arches. "Does it smell like…" He sniffs the air. "Sex… in here?"

"What are you talking about?" I blurt out a little too fast to appear nonchalant.

The corner of his mouth twitches as he bites back a smile. He strolls into my office, stopping a foot short of my desk. He kicks out the toe of his shoe, encountering a solid surface.

"Ow," Charlie says softly.

"When did you get red sole Louboutin's?" Trey arches an eyebrow.

I roll my eyes and huff, knowing he's caught me.

"Hey Charlie. Nice shoes. Next time, you might want to make sure they're not sticking out the bottom of the desk."

"Hi Trey," Charlie says from beneath the desk.

"So, what are you doing down there, Charlie?" Trey muses.

"Just looking for something I dropped."

Trey looks up at me, making a blowjob gesture with this hand and mouth.

I shake my head and reach down to help Charlie off the floor. Just as she's about to crawl out, a voice draws my attention to the doorway.

Frank from HR pokes his head in before entering my office. "Bennett, you got a few minutes?"

"Uh… um…" Feeling at a loss for words since I have Charlie under my desk and my belt buckle undone, I am kind of preparing myself for an HR nightmare, but luckily Trey's quick wit saves my ass.

"Frank. Bennett has some paperwork to finish up. But why don't you tell me about that golf trip. Palm Springs, was it?" Trey throws his arm over Frank's shoulder and escorts him out of my office.

When the door closes, my shoulders drop in relief. Damn, that was a close one. I roll my chair back and help Charlie to her feet and sit her on my desk.

"Oh, my god. I can't believe that just happened." She throws her head back in laughter.

"That was close." My hands glide across her soft skin along the outside of her knees and up to her thighs. "We need to be more careful. I don't want anyone seeing what's mine. Plus, I'm sure they wouldn't be too happy knowing this is how we're spending company time."

"You're right. Next time, I'll be sure to lock the door." She gives me a playful wink.

"You naughty girl."

CHAPTER TWENTY-FIVE

A new purpose in life

Charlie

The gravel crunches beneath my tires as I turn into Bennett's driveway. We agreed to meet here, then go to his sister's for Sunday dinner together. Before stepping out of my car, I inhale a few deep breaths to slow my erratic heartbeat. It's not like I haven't met someone's parents before. But this time feels different. We can't keep our hands off each other when we're together, and I can't stop thinking about him when we're apart. I know I tend to wear my heart on my sleeve, but it's never felt like butterflies taking flight inside my stomach every time someone mentions his name. Or my pulse instantly quickens when I see him walk into a room. He just makes me feel good about myself, unlike my ex Jared. And while I enjoyed Kaleb's company, it never felt like this.

As my feet touch the ground, I hold my hand over my eyes to block the warm sun. The smell of lilac wafts through the air. I gaze to the left and then the right, wanting to pinpoint where the scent is coming from. Just a few feet away from the house stands a luscious lilac bush, the warmer fall weather causing them to bloom again. I make a mental note to cut a few branches off to bring over to his sister's. I hope he has a vase.

"Hey gorgeous. I thought I heard you pull in," Bennett yells from his covered porch. He jogs the few steps down and greets me in the driveway.

"I love this dress on you." Bennett looks me up and down before wrapping his arms around my waist and pulls me into him. His finger grazes my temple as he tucks a strand of hair behind my ear. An electric current courses through my body from his light touch.

"Thank you. Maybe later you can take it off." I look up into his eyes, the bright sun causing the blue in his irises to swirl like waves in the ocean.

"With pleasure." Bennett bends down to place a kiss on my lips and then his cheek is flush with mine, his breath caresses my ear. "Or we can skip dinner and get right to the getting naked part."

A throaty laugh escapes, and I playfully slap his chest. "Oh no, mister. This was your idea, so we are going to have dinner. I'm going to ask your family for all the embarrassing stories, maybe even ask for photos. I like a good visual."

"Can't blame me for trying." A boyish grin forms on his lips while taking a few backwards steps towards his truck.

"Wait! I made a pie to bring over." Whirling around, I open the backdoor. "I hope everyone likes apple. Also, do you have a vase?"

As soon as we open the door to his sister's modest split-level house, the aroma of marinara sauce, basil, and oregano fill my nostrils. Within seconds of entering, everyone is there to greet us. They must have known Bennett was bringing a guest. Their eagerness to meet me is evident. Bennett's stepdad,

Dean, shakes my hand first. His salt and pepper hair gives him a sexy older man vibe. Caroline, Bennett's mom, wraps her arms around me in a giant bear hug. One that only a mom can give, it's comforting. Her mahogany colored hair smells of lavender. Liana, a spitting image of her brother, minus the eye color, instantly welcomes me with a hug. I pass her the large drinking glass full of lilacs explaining Bennett didn't have a vase. She inhales the scent, telling me that lilacs are her favorite and pulls me in for another hug. Her husband, Mark, stretches out his hand for me to shake, just as their two kids round the corner to investigate all the commotion while clinging tight to Mark.

I bend down to introduce myself. They're shy at first but quickly warm up to me and insist on showing me all their toys. Shortly after the first round of introductions, a couple of Bennett's aunts and uncles arrive, along with a few of his cousins. Bennett has his arm around my shoulder, holding me tight while everyone talks amongst each other. Their family dynamic is something I could get used to. It's loud and chaotic. My lips pull into a full smile. A sense of envy passes through me. I never got this growing up. Maybe I can have this with Bennett?

After introductions, we sit down for the most delicious dinner I think I've ever eaten. Sunday dinners might be my new favorite activity. They gobble up my whole pie. Dean even had two pieces. Once we clean our plates, I volunteer me and Bennett to wash the dishes.

A fire burns in the stone fire pit as we gather on the back patio overlooking a rolling field. Oranges, pinks, and purples paint the sky as the sun dips below the horizon.

"So, what was it like growing up with Bennett?" I ask Liana.

"Growing up with my baby brother…" She peers up at the sky and taps her chin.

"You say it like you're so much older than me." Bennett

shifts his attention towards me. "Eighteen months. That's all that separates us."

"But I'm still older," Liana singsongs. "Bennett was a really great brother. He did everything he could to help us."

Something about the way she said the last part has me wondering what happened. I'll have to ask Bennett about that later.

"Oh, here's a story for you Charlie." Liana leans forward. "I was about six and Bennett was five. We were out shopping with Mom, and she had to pee, so she brought us to the bathroom stall with her. While Mom was doing her business, Bennett starts crawling under all the stalls, saying hi to all the other women using the restroom."

An eruption of laughter fills the patio. Directing my attention to Bennett. "So, you were a ladies man even back then?" He just smirks and shrugs his shoulders.

"I was so embarrassed. After that I contemplated hanging a sign around his neck that said, 'free to a good home'," Caroline replies. Another round of laughter sounds around us.

"Or how about that one time—" Liana continues.

"Okay, okay, enough of the 'let's embarrass Bennett' stories. I'm trying not to scare this one off." Bennett wraps his arm around me and hugs me tight as we sit on the two person bench.

After the sun has set and the stars litter the night sky, I continue to listen to his family share stories of them all growing up. Liana even had a few baby pictures of Bennett saved on her phone. She showed me one of him wearing an adorable cowboy costume complete with a red hat, belt buckle, and boots with spurs.

"You make a pretty cute cowboy," I say to Bennett.

"My mom might still have that costume. I could find it and we can play dress up." He wiggles his eyebrows.

"Oh my god, now that would be a sight to see."

After polishing off a few more drinks and sharing more stories that I definitely won't let Bennett live down, Liana and Mark go inside to tuck the kids into bed as we say goodbye to Caroline and Dean.

"Hey, let's go for a walk." Bennett reaches for my hand and tugs me behind him.

"Uh, it's dark out there and something might eat me." My voice trembles.

"Don't worry, I'll protect you," Bennett whispers against the shell of my ear.

The way Bennett says it sends a jolt of passion through me. I wrap my arm around his as we make our way down a moonlit path. The rustling of leaves float through the air as the lights from the house becoming a speckle in the distance.

"You're not taking me out here to kill me, are you?"

"No." A hearty laugh escapes his belly. "Just something I want to show you. I think you'll like it."

I nod, even though Bennett can't see me. On the horizon, a silhouette of a building begins to take shape against the dark backdrop. When we're close enough, Bennett takes a step up and holds up my hand to guide me inside. As soon as I stride passed him, Bennett bends down and seconds later, the entire space illuminates with a soft glow from the Edison string lights twinkling amidst the inky sky.

"This gazebo is gorgeous." I gaze up at the lights on the perimeter of the roof. I let my hand float across the painted white railing then I come to a halt. A trellis of white climbing hydrangeas greets me. My fingertips caressing the silky, smooth leaves. I lean in, inhaling, as the floral scent permeates my nose.

"I knew you would love this." Bennett's deep voice from over my shoulder pulls me out of my trance.

Turning to Bennett. "I do. I want one."

"I'll work on building you whatever you want." He pulls me into his chest and softly places a kiss on top of my head.

He gently rocks us back and forth as if soft music was playing in the gazebo.

"So, we've established your name isn't Charlotte, where did Charlie come from?"

With his arms still wrapped around me, I exhale a small laugh. "For whatever reason, my parents decided to name me after my grandfather. While my mom was pregnant, they were convinced I was a boy, so they picked out the name. But then I was born and surprise, not a boy. They decided to keep the name anyway. Also, where did the Charlotte come from?"

His chest vibrates with laughter, causing me to pull away and look up at him. "That first time I saw you, I was so enamored by your presence that I lost all ability to think. My brain and my mouth were no longer connected so I just spewed the first thing that came out. Charlie is often a nickname for Charlotte, I went with it. Clearly, I was wrong."

"But you kept calling me that even after I corrected you."

"Yeah. I was a jackass for that. You were the distraction I didn't need so I thought if I could make you hate me it would be easier than fighting my own temptations. Unfortunately, I found it more of a turn on when you would get flustered with me."

Playfully, I push him away. "You're such an ass. You found enjoyment in making me mad."

He reaches for me and tugs me back to him and I go willingly. "Plus, you were with what's his face but if I knew then what I know now I would have totally stolen you away from him."

"Oh, you think I would have just ditched him to be with you?"

"I think you would find it hard to resist my charm."

"So full of yourself."

"For what it's worth, I'm sorry for being a jerk. What do I have to do for you to forgive me?"

I give him a sultry smile. "I could think of a few things."

"Anything." His head bends down as I look up to him and he places a chaste kiss on my lips. "I've never met a girl like you, Charlie. Sure, I dated here and there, but none of them held my attention like you. I feel like I have a new purpose in life."

"And what's that?" I look up into his glimmering blue eyes.

A smile tugs at his lips. "You."

"And what was the old purpose?"

Bennett pulls away and moves to lean against the railing, his hands gripping the top as if it's his lifeline. His eyes wander to the ceiling and a deep breath escapes his lungs.

"We may seem like a pretty tight knit family but growing up was hard. We did the best we could." Bennett pauses as if to collect his thoughts. "When I was around six years old, our father left us. He was messing around on my mom and decided he didn't want this family anymore; he wanted the other one."

"I'm so sorry." I rest my hand on his arm for comfort.

"It's okay. If he didn't want to be with us, we didn't want him around. So, it was just me, my mom, and Liana. Granted, my sister is older, but I still felt like I had to look after her and my mom. Step up and be the man of the house."

My heart aches for this little boy who had to grow up too fast.

Bennett continues. "My mom worked two jobs to keep a roof over our head and food on the table. As soon as I was old enough, I got an after-school job to help take some of the burden off my mom." Bennett pushes off the railing to stand in front of me. "My junior year of high school, my mom met Dean. He did everything he could to care for us. He took the burden off me and actually offered me a job at his real estate company during the summer. Mostly just office grunt work, but now and then he would show me the more hands on stuff. From there, my interest in real estate came to fruition. I always kept the work mentality, feeling the need to provide for my family. That's why my sister has been on my case about settling down. She wants me to take care of myself for once instead of everyone else."

"Oh wow. I never would have guessed. I always knew you were a hard worker. You always seemed so determined." I wrap my arms around his waist and press my cheek to his hard chest, feeling the thump of his heartbeat.

"Looking back, I wouldn't change anything. Who knows, I may have never met you." His hand reaches up to tilt my head, so his eyes meet mine.

"A part of me likes to think we would've found each other."

After a few passing beats, Bennett asks, "What's your story? You grew up around here, right?"

"I did. Well, a couple hours away. Growing up was kinda lonely. I'm an only child and while my parents provided me with the basic needs, they weren't there when I needed their love and support. They were always busy chasing the next big thing." I take a deep breath. "They were never in the audience during school concerts or never came to any of my sporting games. I just got used to it. I try not to resent them, but it's hard. I talk to them every now and then but we're not close like your family. My friends became my family. So, when a high school friend moved here for college, I decided to tag along. Worked a few odd jobs here and there until I was hired at The Blue Stone Group. Met the cheating boyfriend and you know the rest of the story." I release a small chuckle.

"He didn't know what he had. His loss along with that other guy. If I were him, I wouldn't have left."

I stretch up on my tippy toes, pressing a kiss to his mouth. The taste of beer lingers on his lips. His arms wrap around my waist pulling me closer.

"Now that I have you. I'm never letting you go." His words are a whisper against my lips.

A crack of thunder in the distance pulls us from our tender moment. We spend a few minutes watching the lightning storm brew in front of us.

"We better get going. The storm looks like it's approaching fast." Bennett pushes off from the railing.

"I wasn't expecting rain today. It was such a beautiful day."

"Yeah, me either," Bennett says at the same time a lightning bolt lights up the black sky along with another roar of thunder.

Just then, rain drops pebble down on the roof. Bennett grabs my hand, flips the light switch off, and we jog back to the house, the sparks of lightning illuminating our way down the path.

CHAPTER TWENTY-SIX

Karma's a real bitch

Charlie

My hands tremble while it feels as if my heart is going to jump out of my chest. What could they want to talk to me about? Did Frank see me under Bennett's desk that day? Am I fired? What am I going to do?

Suddenly, Olivia's hand is on my bouncing knee. "You need to calm down. I'm sure it's nothing. Maybe they want to give you a raise. New position? Your own office?"

When I walked into work Friday morning, I was greeted with an email stating HR wants a meeting with me. As soon as I read those words, my heart dropped. I began pacing around the small area behind the desk, unsure of what to do while I wait. Olivia came in and was my voice of reason and got me to sit down. The ringing phone jolts me from my thoughts. My hand trembles as I place the receiver to my ear. Frank's voice is on the other end, his words short and clipped. When the call ends, I set the phone back down.

My heart is thumping wildly in my chest as I turn toward Olivia. "That was HR."

"You got this girl. If they fire you, I'm gone too."

My lips pull into a half smile. "I appreciate your loyalty, but you don't need to do that."

"Oh, good." Olivia sighs in relief. "But know, just say the word, and I will."

"Wish me luck." I'm praying for more than luck as an enormous knot forms in my stomach.

Standing to my full height and squaring my shoulders, I stride toward the elevator. Nervous energy surges through my body as I'm preparing myself to get fired. I'm lucky to have a little in savings that can tide me over for a bit. I stop in front of the elevator and press the button and watch as it lights up. The doors immediately open as if they were waiting for me. I step over the threshold and press the button for the second floor. The doors close and my heart rate spikes.

I feel as if I'm sweating through my shirt. I use the mirrored interior to check under my arms. Still dry. The back of my head hits the wall with a thud as my shoulders slump. This is all I've ever done, I love my job, and I work with my two best friends. I'm never going to get this again.

The elevator glides to a stop and the doors open. Bright light fills the atrium from the rising sun as I step out, turn right, ready to accept the consequences. Is this what it feels like to walk to your death? As I pass closed door after closed door, "The Imperial March" plays over and over in my head. My stride slows as I come to a halt, Human Resources engraved on the wall plate. My eyes follow the wood grain of the dark stained door. I raise my hand and rap my knuckle at the spot my eyes were just fixated on.

A muffled voice on the other side informs me to come in. With slow precision, my fingers turn the brass handle and step inside the doorway, ready to face my fate.

"What's happening? I got the 9-1-1 message and ran right here!" Parisa throws herself into the booth of a quiet Porter's.

My forehead rests on the cool, slightly sticky, wood tabletop as Olivia rubs my back. "She got a promotion." Pity laces her voice.

"Promotion? That's great! Congratulations Charlie!" Parisa says.

I raise my head and look her in the eyes. "But it's halfway across the country." My bottom lip juts out as I whine.

I showed up at the meeting already accepting my fate, but I was completely wrong. They didn't catch me and Bennett. I wasn't about to be fired. Instead, they wanted to give me a raise and a promotion. But that also came with some stipulations. Since The Blue Stone Group was expanding, they needed someone to head the new office, and they thought I would be perfect for the position.

Parisa's eyes go wide. "Oh... I see."

"But you're not fired, so that's a bonus," Olivia says.

Turning toward Olivia as I give her the death glare, I scoff. "At this point I would rather be fired. Now, I have to decide if I want to move to Colorado and have this amazing job opportunity and leave you guys and Bennett or stay here and wonder what if." My head bobbles back and forth while I try to capture my straw with my mouth. When I catch that little bastard, I suck until my cheeks dimple. With the straw still in my mouth, I mumble, "I don't think I'm going to get this kind of opportunity here. This could be my only chance to further my career in this company." I suck again, that annoying slurping sound becoming louder when I hit the last sip at the bottom of my drink.

Olivia's hand shoots up to get the waitress's attention. Round three, here we go!

Leaning in as if afraid someone might hear, Parisa asks, "Did you tell Bennett?"

My arms flail above me before crashing down on the table.

"Tell Bennett? No! What am I supposed to say? Oh, we just started this amazing relationship, but hey I'm leaving now."

"Hey sweetie..." Olivia says as if talking to a child. "You're about here." She raises her hand above her head and brings it down to her chest. "But I need you here. It's not quite late enough to show your drunkenness."

I sob onto the table. This table is the only thing that cares.

Parisa reaches over and clasps her hand on top of mine. "Maybe he'll go with you?"

Why does this conversation sound so familiar? Oh, wait, it's the same one I had previously with Kaleb. Karma, you're a real bitch.

The waitress reappears, and I snatch my drink off her tray before she can set it down. The rest of the night carries on. One margarita after the other. I should really buy stock in tequila. Oh! Start my own tequila farm. But I'd have to move to Mexico.

"Guys! Let's move to Mexico!" I blurt out. "We can buy some land and plant those things that look like pineapples but aren't and make tequila. But it must be tequila. Not mezcal with the worm. That gives me the willies." A shudder racks through my body.

A pair of strong, masculine hands grip my biceps, startling me, almost causing me to spill my drink. His signature citrus and leather scent wafts to my nose. At that moment, I know exactly who's behind me. His warm breath tickles my ear. "Hey beautiful. Looks like you've made friends with Jose tonight."

"The best of friends." I gaze into his deep ocean blue eyes.

Bennett reaches around the side of the booth and grabs my bag and tucks me into his side. "Let's get you home to sleep off some of this tequila."

CHAPTER TWENTY-SEVEN

Margarita's one. Bennett zero.

Bennett

I was at my sister's house when I got a text message. I had to wrangle my phone back from my niece and nephew to see it was a message from Olivia using Charlie's number. Charlie had a few too many drinks and was talking about moving to Mexico so I should come pick her up. I heard through the grapevine that Charlie had a rough day and a meeting with HR, so I wanted to give her space to figure everything out. Olivia mentioned they were going to have a girls' night. I figured Charlie would come to me when she was ready.

When I open the door to Porter's, I'm greeted by a sea of people. I shuffle through the crowd until I reach their regular booth. My gaze instantly lands on Charlie. Her back facing me, her long, chestnut hair cascading in waves down her back. I place my hands on her biceps. "Let's get you home and sleep off some of this tequila."

After I collect her purse, I give her my hand to help her up. I hold out her sweater so she can put her arms through the sleeves. As we walk toward the exit, she flings her hand above her head, dramatically waving to everyone. Once outside the brisk, cool air hits her skin, and I feel her shiver. I wrap my arms around her shoulder as she wraps hers around my waist, snuggling closer for warmth. The path to my truck only illuminated by a single lap post.

"Food. I need food." A whine escapes her lips. "Fries. Delicious salty goodness."

I try to hold back my laugh but fail. "Oh, I could give you some salty goodness." A loud smack echoes through the parking lot from a back hand to the stomach and I double over with an 'oomph' followed by a wheezing laugh. "Alright, when we get home, I'll make you one of my famous sandwiches."

"With french fries?"

"I'll see what I can make happen."

A soft rumble sounds from the tires as we pull into my gravel driveway. With my truck in park, I step out and circle around the front. I open the passenger door, turn around, and bend at the knees. "Hop on."

"Wait, like a piggyback ride?"

"Yeah." I nod my head, motioning for her to hop on.

"I haven't had one of these in years!"

She reaches around my shoulders, clasping her hands together. I pull her legs tight around my waist and stand.

"Wait! My fries!"

While on the drive back to my place, we passed a fast-food joint. Charlie's face was glued to the window, and I was convinced she was going to jump out of the moving vehicle to get fries, so I circled back to enter the drive thru.

After she grabs her fries, I carry her up to the house, only the dim moonlight lighting our way. When we reach the short stairs to the porch, a motion light flickers to life. Charlie's body slides down my back as I fish the keys from my pocket. Unlocking the door, I hold it open as she steps through. She flicks the light switch as if this was her own house, illuminating the foyer. The thought of her living in my space sends a warmth coursing through my body. I follow her to the right as she hobbles through the house, toeing off her shoes, leaving a trail to the kitchen. The bag crinkles as she digs in to grab another fry, unable to resist the aroma of grease and salt.

My eyes train on her as she wiggles up on a bar stool while trying to maintain her balance and not lose her bag of fries. She releases a small huff. "We need to talk." A somber tone laces her voice.

"We'll talk tomorrow. When the tequila has left your body." A part of me already knows what this conversation will be since I overheard Frank discussing the new candidates for the promotion.

"Tequila. Did I tell you I'm going to start a tequila farm? The rolling hills will be covered with not pineapple plants." Her hand waves in front of her, demonstrating her vast, rolling hills.

"Agave plants?"

Her finger darts out to point at me. "Yes, those!"

Reaching for her bag, she pops another fry into her mouth. This time, my eyes dart to her fingers as she slowly licks the salt off each digit.

"You going to share?"

"Maybe…" Her hand goes back into the bag and pulls out another fry. Just before it reaches her lips, she loses her grip, and it tumbles down into the cleavage of her shirt.

I bark out a laugh as she goes fishing for her lost fry. Her eyes widen with delight, triumph written on her face as she pulls it out and holds it up in the air.

"Found it!" Then pointing it in my direction, she asks, "Do you want the boob fry?"

"Those are the best fries." I lean over the concrete

countertop, my eyes fixated on hers, stealing it from her fingers with my mouth. A lustful gaze fills her eyes as she climbs up on the counter and struts towards me on her hands and knees. She stops in front of me, sitting back on her haunches, her feather light touch caresses my cheeks.

I lean into her touch before kissing her pouty lips, the taste of salt still lingering on them. My hands thread through her silky locks, deepening the kiss. She releases a moan, exposing her sun kissed tanned skin to me as I place kisses across her jaw, down to her neck, alternating between sucking and little bites. She adjusts her position, so I'm nestled between her legs. I haul her to me as her legs wrap around my waist.

With her hot breath against my ear she whispers, "You know what goes well with fries?"

"What's that?"

"A hard. Throbbing. Cock."

A laugh escapes me. "Cock and fries. Sounds like a well-balanced diet."

Her hand roams down to my bulge and caresses me through my pants. "Even better when it's yours." Her voice is low and husky.

"Good to know." I tuck a loose strand of hair behind ear and whisper, "But see, I like something a little more sweeter, like this pussy of yours." Gripping her hips, I tug so she's pressed up against my erection. "If I put my mouth between your legs, how many licks would it take to make you come?"

"I don't know but we should find out."

"You don't need to tell me twice."

Lifting her up, I hurriedly make my way through the house to get to my bedroom. Taking the stairs two at a time. And the whole time Charlie's soft lips are on my neck, driving me wild. I know she's drunk and I should get her to sleep, but she started this. I'm just a willing participant.

Finally, making it to the bedroom, I toss Charlie on the bed, and she lets out a squeal. I pull my shirt over my head as

Charlie's hooded eyes watch me like I'm her last meal. I start to unbutton my pants but stop and look down at Charlie.

"Your turn."

She tears off her clothes like she's trying to win a get naked race. When I'm down to my boxer briefs, I crawl onto the bed, hovering over her. My eyes scan her face, her slightly upturned nose, full pink lips, my fingers trace a scar over her eyebrow.

"You are the best thing that's happened to me, Charlie. My life wasn't complete until you."

Before she can respond, I kiss her. My tongue traces her lips, coaxing her to open for me. Our tongues stroke and caress one another. I grind my hardening cock into the apex of her thighs as nails drag down my back, no doubt leaving a trail of red marks.

"Please fuck me, Bennett." Charlie's husky voice spurs me on.

Reaching over to the nightstand drawer, I blindly search for a condom. But my search comes up empty. Damn. I break the kiss and a soft whimper escapes Charlie.

"Be right back. I gotta find a condom."

With no hesitancy, I haul ass into the master bathroom, opening drawer after drawer, determined to find a condom. I must have one hidden in here somewhere. I tear open the zipper of my Dopp kit, a gold foil packet sitting on top. I feel like I just won the lottery. Grabbing it, I flip it over with my fingers. Not expired. I run back to the bedroom, condom in hand like I won a gold medal.

Only when I reach the bed, a soft snore comes from Charlie's slightly parted lips. I toss the condom into the drawer. Ultimately, our night has come to an end. Tugging the blanket over Charlie, I place a kiss on her forehead before climbing onto the other side.

Margaritas one.

Bennett zero.

CHAPTER TWENTY-EIGHT

Too good to be true

Charlie

My head throbs like it's in a vise grip and someone is slowly turning the handle, tightening it with each pass. I'm never drinking again. *Famous last words.* I roll over, groaning as I crack an eye. The mid-morning light shines through the partially open drapes, casting a sun beam right on the comforter hitting me directly in the face. I groan again and roll over away from the offending light, wrapping the blanket around my head like a fur-lined parka.

Bennett tugs part of the blanket away from my face. "Hey, how are you feeling?"

"Like death," I groan.

"Tequila will do that to you. I have some aspirin and water here for you. I gotta run to my sister's and help Mark with something. I'll be back in a bit. Help yourself to anything."

He leans down, his soft lips press to my forehead. A low whimper escapes, wanting him to come back to bed, but instead I hear the soft click of the door shutting. A few minutes tick by as yesterday's events run through my head.

HR meeting. Job promotion. Margaritas. So many margaritas. Slapping myself on the forehead. I still need to talk to Bennett. Since he'll be gone for a few hours, maybe I can compose myself, so I don't look and feel like the walking dead.

I pop the two aspirin into my mouth and guzzle down the water, so thankful for Bennett's thoughtfulness. I wonder where my phone is. Reluctantly, I toss the covers off and roll out of bed to go on a mission to find my phone. Once the cool air hits my skin, I look down. *Where are my clothes?* My eyes scan the floor, but when I look up, I spot a partially closed door.

Tugging on the door handle, I flick on the light. A bright light illuminates an expansive walk-in closet. All his work suits on one side and his everyday wear on the other. I head in that direction and find a thread bare t-shirt with Harbor Highlands College on the front. The fresh laundered scent mixed with his own citrus leathery scent permeates my nostrils as I tug the shirt over my head. I bring the neckline up to my nose, inhaling deeply. I love his smell. Now, not feeling so naked, I continue my mission to find my phone.

First, my eyes dart to the nightstand and then the dresser along the wall, but no luck. A few articles of my clothes scatter across the floor, but no phone. *I wonder if I left it downstairs.* My hand glides along the railing as my feet descend the wooden staircase. At the bottom, I turn right and pass through the dining room. Before I fully enter the kitchen, I spot a black cell phone shaped object sitting on the counter. Bingo! There's my phone. I quicken my pace, but when I pick it up and turn it over, I notice it's not mine but Bennett's. I'll just use his phone to find mine.

My fingers dance across the screen as I type in his passcode and the screen lights up. A smile tugs on my lips as I see his home screen is a picture of us. I remember that day vividly. We were out for a walk by the lake when I told him I wanted to stop for a selfie. We were standing side by side all smiles when we saw a Jack Russell Terrier trying to hump a Husky and we both busted out laughing. Bennett just so happened to snap a picture at that moment.

A flash on the screen catches my attention. A notification. Not wanting to snoop around on my boyfriend's phone, I ignore it, but then an icon at the top catches my eye. The FLIRT app. Why does he still have the app? My heart rate spikes. Is he talking to other girls? We never talked about deleting it. I just assumed we would when he said he wanted to be exclusive. Is he another Jared? My finger fumbles as I swipe down to see a preview of the notification. Staring back at me is a message.

HottieKim: Hey Stud ;) You free tonight?

What the fuck? Abandoning my no snooping idea, I go full on detective. Without a second thought, I return to the home screen, find the app, and open it. Instantly, I'm greeted with message after message of *Hey Sexy, I like your eyes, I'm down for a good time, how about you, I got your message the other night,* and then the one that originally drew my attention. *Hey Stud ;) You free tonight?*

The phone clatters down on to the countertop. That mother fucking cheating asshole. A flurry of rage courses through me. How could he do this? He is just like that scumbag Jared. Of course, I couldn't find a good guy for once. Or maybe I did, and I let him go to San Francisco alone. I'm such an idiot. I bolt out of the kitchen wanting to collect my stuff and get the hell out of here but stop dead in my tracks. Fuck! I don't have my car. I don't know where my phone is. Pivoting on my heel, I stomp back to the counter, swipe Bennett's phone, and call mine. My faint ring tone sounds from upstairs. I scurry back up the stairs, already tired of this hide and go seek game with my phone. I press redial as I enter Bennett's bedroom. Begrudgingly, I get down on the floor and belly crawl under the bed to retrieve it. I toss Bennett's phone on the bed as my fingers fly over the screen of mine. After a few rings, the phone connects.

"Can you come pick me up at Bennett's?"

CHAPTER TWENTY-NINE

Operation Bennett's a dumbass, but loves Charlie

Bennett

When I arrive home, I am greeted with an empty house. Charlie's gone. Her clothes are no longer on my floor. Her shoe trail is missing from the hallway. My phone, which I forgot in the kitchen when I left, is now sitting on my bed. When I unlock the screen, the FLIRT app is pulled up, showing message after message from various women. What the fuck? I close the app and I dial her number and it goes straight to voicemail. I dial again. Voicemail. Getting irritated, I hit redial once more. Voicemail again, but this time I leave a message.

Didn't I delete the app? And why were all those women suddenly sending me messages? I haven't been on that app since the last time I messaged Charlie. Fuck! I turn around, my fist connecting with my bedroom door. The skin on my knuckles split open. Drops of red dot my hand. I grab my phone, and dial Olivia. A few rings pass before a voice picks up.

"Hello?"

"Where's Charlie?"

Olivia's voice goes to a hushed whisper. "She's here, but it's not a—"

"Let me talk to her." My voice more stern this time.

"Now's not a good time. Give her some time. She'll come around." Dead air fills the other end.

God dammit! I hurl my phone, watching it fly into a million pieces as it hits the wall. Fuck! Now, I need a new phone.

I jog down the stairs two at a time, grab my keys, and slam the front door. When I reach my truck, I jam the key into the ignition and slam it into drive. The tires kick up a trail of dust and rocks as I fishtail out of the driveway.

My tires squeal on the pavement as I turn left into Trey's neighborhood. I pass house after house, my speedometer reading well over the speed limit. When I arrive at his house, I come to a screeching halt in his driveway. My door is barely shut by the time I'm pounding on Trey's front door. Growing more impatient with each passing second he doesn't answer, I bang harder. The door flies open, and Trey's body fills the wood frame.

"Hey man, what's the deal? What did my door do to you?"

"Where does Olivia live? Everyone knows you've been fucking around with her. I'm sure you've been to her place."

"What the fuck does that mean?"

Feeling defeated, I let out a sigh, my adrenaline falling. "I fucked up. And Charlie's gone."

Trey steps out of the doorway and signals for me to come inside. I step over the threshold and amble into the living room, collapsing onto his dark brown leather sectional. Trey takes a seat on the other side and asks, "Dude, what happened?"

I rest my elbows on my knees, my hands rake through my hair. "I don't know. She stayed at my place last night. This morning I went to Liana's house for a few hours and when I came back, she was gone. But here's the kicker, my phone was on the bed with the FLIRT app open and messages from other women."

"You dog! You've been chatting with other women?"

"Fuck no! I don't even know why they messaged me. I thought I deleted the app months ago. But apparently not. I can't lose her, man. She's the best thing that's happened to me."

"Those are some big words to be throwing out there."

"When I'm not with her, I'm thinking about her. When I'm with her, I'm thinking about her. She's my world. And then there was the job promotion offer we never talked about, but I knew about it. Fuck! This is the perfect reason for her to take it."

"Where's your phone?"

"In pieces on my bedroom floor.

"Well, shit… hold that thought." Trey gets up and walks out of the room. After a few minutes, he returns with his MacBook. He tosses it onto the cushion next to me. "Use this. Log into your account. Let's see what the messages say."

"I don't give a shit about the messages."

"No, you asshole. It's to see if we can figure out why they messaged you." I side eye Trey but grab the laptop and log in any way. The cushion next to me dips as Trey takes a seat. "Also, just so you know; Olivia and I have never hooked up. Hell, we haven't even kissed."

"What do you mean?"

"One night when I drove her home, I was being a gentleman and walked her to her door. She turned to me, and I was convinced she was going to kiss me. She rose on her toes, leaned in, then dodged left and kissed my cheek. My cheek."

I look up from the computer screen as it loads. "That must have been a blow to your ego."

Trey shrugs one shoulder. "No worries about my ego. I

went down to Porter's and found a hot brunette to blow it." A face-splitting grin covers his face.

I release a hearty laugh. "Dude, your time is coming. Just wait."

"Never." Trey shakes his head.

Once the web page is loaded, Trey leans over to get a better view. My cursor hovers over the message button before I click to open the mailbox. Jesus Christ. Over ten new messages, all within the last twenty-four hours. No wonder Charlie hates me. I would hate me too if I found this on my phone.

"Click on that one." Trey points to the screen. "She looks hot."

I smack his hand away. "That's not why we're here."

I start at the top and open the message.

Adonis21: HIYAAAAA

HottieKim: Hey Stud ;)

"I didn't write that." I move the cursor to the next message and click.

Adonis21: wiekaid ejejej *eggplant emoji, pizza emoji, banana emoji, rainbow emoji*

Amber44: Hey Sexy, I like your eyes

"Dude, were you drunk?" Trey asks.

I click on the next.

Adonis21: *eggplant emoji, banana emoji, unicorn emoji*

Jenny99: I'm down for a good time. How about you?

I stare at Trey's laptop in disbelief. "I never wrote any of these."

"Did someone hack your account? Someone use your phone?"

After a long pause, it hits me. Fuck. The other night when I was at my sister's. I place the laptop on the couch next to me and rake my hands down my face. "My niece and nephew were playing with my phone the other night. They must have hit some buttons and sent those random ass messages."

"Damn. Chalk that up as another reason to never have kids."

I rest my elbows on my knees and look up at Trey. "What am I going to do? This is the one girl I actually care about. And now I've just fucked it all up."

"Yeah, she probably thinks you're just like her ex."

My eyes bore into Trey. "Not helping."

Trey rubs his hands together and stands. "Alright, let's win your girl back! Let 'Operation Bennett's a dumbass but loves Charlie' commence."

Love… do I love Charlie? I can't love Charlie. But she's all I think about as soon as I wake up. Her dazzling smile and friendly eyes. The cute way she sticks her tongue out just a little when she's concentrating really hard. How she separates her Skittles into colors and then eats them in groups, so she doesn't taint the distinct flavor of each candy. I think I love this girl.

I rise to my feet next to Trey and puff out my chest. "I love Charlie!"

"Yeah, I know. That's why I said it." Trey rolls his eyes and digs for his phone in his pocket and exits the room, mumbling under his breath. "Doesn't anyone ever listen to me? I'm more than just a pretty face…"

"Hey where are you going?" I turn on my heel and chase after Trey. He waves his hand at me, halting my progress. All

I hear is yeah, yeah, fucking idiot, okay, he loves her, okay, yeah. He spins around, phone still to his ear.

"Who was that?" I spit out before Trey has the chance to hang up.

"That was Olivia. Got some bad news, man. Charlie wants to saw off your nuts and dangle them from her rearview mirror like a pair of fuzzy dice."

My forehead crinkles. "Did she really say that?"

"I was paraphrasing. But it doesn't sound good."

"There must be something I can do. Anything. She can't leave it like this. She has to talk to me," I plead.

Trey's somber gaze drifts to mine. "I don't know. This might be the end."

CHAPTER THIRTY

Guess I was wrong

Charlie

I didn't know my feet could move so fast. As soon as I saw all those messages on Bennett's phone, my heart dropped. I raced around his house, collected everything I could and left. My car was still at Porter's, so I had to leave on foot. Waiting for Olivia was not an option. If Bennett arrived back, I couldn't face him. Tears well in my eyes. How could this happen again? What did I do to deserve this? I must have been a real bitch in another life.

The beeping of a car horn draws my attention and I turn around, shielding my eyes from the harsh sun to see Olivia's silver Audi Q7. When the rumble of the tires as they hit the gravel on the shoulder, I step out of the way so she can pull up next to me. I throw open the door, toss my bag into the back, slide into the smooth leather seat, and slam the door behind me.

I sulk in my seat as Olivia steps on the gas, understanding my need to get out of here. A few quiet minutes pass then Olivia breaks the silence.

"You alright?"

A lone tear falls down my cheek, followed by another, unable to hold them back any longer. "I really thought it was going to be different this time. That I actually found a good guy. Guess I was wrong." I swipe away the moisture.

"Aww honey. I'm sorry. We all thought he was a good guy."

I throw my hands up in the air. "How could I have fallen for him? Sure, he seemed so charming and acted like he cared for me, but then there were all those other girls." I slump down in the seat as the tears start to fall again. "What's wrong with me? Am I that unlovable?" My shoulders shake with each sob that pours out of me.

Olivia throws the car into park as soon as she's in her driveway and turns toward me. She reaches for my hands and looks me in the eyes. "Charlie, this is not your fault. Understand me? He's the asshole."

I swipe at my tears.

"Let's get you inside. I'll make us some food. You can shower and we'll veg out, okay?"

All I can do is nod as she grabs my bag from the back before we walk the path to the house.

I follow Olivia into her sleek modern kitchen. She opens her white Café french door refrigerator, pulls out a water, and places the plastic bottle in front of me.

Olivia tilts her head. "Are you wearing his shirt?"

I look down. Dammit. I threw his shirt on while I was looking for mine and forgot I had it on.

"His stupid shirt, with all its stupid holes." I poke a finger through the torn fabric. "You know, he has an entire closet full of shirts like this. They're all ratty and full of holes. He says he can't get rid of them because they hold sentimental value. Who does that? It's a shirt. Get over it." I twist the cap off the water and take a drink.

"Why don't you go take a shower. Help yourself to some fresh clothes in my closet."

I nod my head and make my way to the staircase. Once I reach the bathroom, I turn the rain shower head on and steam fills the room. I shed my clothes and let the water wash away all my feelings. When I finish, I step out and wrap a towel around me. Wiping the fog off the mirror, I stare back at a girl with red, puffy, and vacant eyes. I deserve better than this. I deserve someone better than this. And I know what I need to do.

The car comes to a stop at the departure terminal doors. I open the door and round the car to the back. The sound of traffic, car horns, and people talking echoes between the buildings. A shiver blast through me as a gust of wind passes through like a wind tunnel. Tugging my coat tighter around me, I meet Parisa at the trunk of her. After she opens it, I heave my suitcase out, setting it on the ground. "Thanks for the ride."

"Anytime. I can't believe you might be leaving us. I don't want to say goodbye."

"It's only a preliminary trip. I'll be back in a few days. They want me to check out the new office and make sure it will be a good fit. But I think a fresh start is exactly what I need. Something must be in the air here because I keep getting burned."

She gives me a sympathetic look. "I'm sorry, Charlie. No one saw this coming. You guys were perfect for each other."

Tears prick my eyes. I've spent too many hours crying over this man. I don't need to start again now. "He had us all fooled." I exhale a deep breath. "Okay, I'm going to get going."

Parisa reaches her arm around me and gives me a big hug. "Safe travels. Keep us updated about the job."

I give her a tight smile and nod before I turn and stride through the double glass sliding doors. I meander through the people as I approach the ticket counter. A middle-aged woman in a sensible blue and white pant suit greets me with a friendly smile. While she checks my travel documents, I lift my suitcase onto the scale.

She hands back by I.D. and boarding pass. "Have a great trip to Aspen."

CHAPTER THIRTY-ONE

You think or you know

Bennett

As I walk into The Blue Stone Group Monday morning, Olivia and Parisa are at the front desk. Instantly, I see the vacant spot next to Olivia. On instinct, my feet rush to the desk. "Where's Charlie?" I ask, panic in my voice.

They share a quick glance before Olivia speaks. "She's in Colorado."

My heart drops to my stomach while disbelief floods my face. "She took the job? She didn't even say anything to me." I run my hands through my hair. "I've been trying to call her all weekend. I left who the fuck knows how many voicemails. I sat outside her apartment for hours, in the cold, until someone threatened to call the cops. I just want her to know it's not what she thinks." My eyes dart between the two women, a pleading look on my face. They must believe me. Someone must believe me.

Parisa reaches over and rests her hand on my forearm. "She just needs some time. In her head you're just like her ex—"

"But I'm not."

Parisa finishes. "But in her mind, you are. She'll be in Colorado for a few days, then she'll be back. Just give her that time."

My shoulders slump and I nod. Turning on my heel, I make my way to the elevator to go to my office. Two days. I'll give her two days, then I'm demanding that she listens to what I have to say because there is no way I am letting her go without a fight.

Piles of paperwork are scattered all over my desk. I've spent the last few hours buried in work so I could stay out of my head. The ringing from my cell phone pulls my attention. Liana's name flashes on the screen and I answer.

"Hey,"

"Hey, baby bro. What are you and Charlie doing tonight? Mark just got a new flat top griddle and needs some taste testers, so burgers tonight. Six p.m."

"Uh, well, Charlie and I aren't together at this moment. Plus, she's in Colorado, possibly taking a new job."

"Wait!" A high pitch screech sounds on the other end. "What do you mean, you're not together? And a job offer? What did you do?"

"Why do you think this is my fault?" Silence fills the air. "Wait, don't answer that. I'll be over and fill you in on everything."

"Yeah, you better! I like Charlie. Don't screw this up for me."

"I'll do what I can just for you." I mumble sarcastically, pressing end on the call, mentally preparing myself for the earful I'm about to get from Liana.

Before I can even raise my hand to knock, Liana throws the door open with a questioning look on her face. "Tell me everything."

"Oh, so nice to see you. I'm doing shitty, by the way. Thanks for asking."

"Haha. I'll get you a beer. You can drown your sorrows in that."

We climb the stairs of the split-level house and I make myself at home, pulling out a stool and taking a seat at the kitchen island. Warm light shines down from the hanging pennants above us. Liana snags a beer from the fridge, twists off the top, and pushes it towards me.

She rests her elbows on the countertop and leans in. "Alright. Tell me what happened."

I reach down and take a swig of my beer before I hash all this out with my sister and have her tell me how much of a fucking idiot I am and that I better not fuck this up. I spend the next twenty minutes telling her my side of the story. That everything is just a big misunderstanding and I'm not like Charlie's asshole ex.

"I can't believe I didn't think of this." Liana plucks my phone out of my hands and taps away at the screen. "Here, this should fix getting any more random messages because of my kids." She hands my phone back to me.

"What did you do?" I stare down at my phone.

"There's an app Mark and I use since the kids always want to play games on our phones. It blocks certain apps and requires a passcode to access them. That way they can only play their games."

"Well, shit. This would have been useful about a week ago."

Liana gives me a sheepish smile. "Sorry, I didn't even think about it. But why didn't you delete the app?"

"I thought I did." My tone a little louder than normal.

"Well, I can't fault her for being mad. I would probably want to junk punch you, too."

"That's all you got? That's your wise words of wisdom?"

Liana releases a soft chuckle. "Someone hurt her once before, and she thinks you did the same thing, so of course her defenses are going to be up. She'll have to talk to you, but she'll need time to digest everything, sort out her own feelings."

"I think I love her."

Liana's eyes look like they're going to bulge out of their sockets. "Those are some big words coming from you. But also, you *think*, or you *know*?"

I take another long pull of my beer, contemplating her question. It's one that's been sitting at the forefront of my mind ever since Trey planted the seed. "I know." A smile tugs at my lips as I say the words. "She's the first girl to ever throw my world off its axis. And now I've managed to fuck it up." My head drops to my phone screen as my fingers fidget with the case.

"I've seen the way she looks at you. She loves you, too. She's just hurting right now."

"But now she might take this job out of state, and then what? Do I just let her go? Pretend none of it was real? Quit my job and follow her?"

She reaches over and places her hand on mine. "Whatever it is, I'm sure you'll make the right decision."

But what if I don't make the right one, and I lose her forever?

CHAPTER THIRTY-TWO

I just need a little more time

Charlie

Colorado was amazing. The views were gorgeous with the Rocky Mountains nestled along the horizon. I don't think I could ever grow tired of it. The driver dropped me off in front of a modern building with sleek lines that houses the new branch of the company. The building isn't as large as the one in Harbor Highlands and the team is much smaller. As I walked through the double glass doors, my potential new boss, Mr. Hendricks, greeted me and whisked me off to show me around, including my own office. I've never had an office before. He had lunch catered in and we discussed my duties and the potential for growth. All of it was a lot to take in, but I know this is an opportunity of a lifetime. One I don't think I can pass up.

But now I'm back in Minnesota and have some tough decisions to make. I drop my bag into the drawer at my desk and before I can even sit, Olivia's perched next to me, anticipation spread across her face. "So how did it go?"

"It went… great."

She scoots her chair closer. "That doesn't sound very convincing."

My eyes fall to the ground, collecting my thoughts before glancing back up at Olivia. "The job is amazing. The location is gorgeous. But I would be leaving you and Parisa."

"And what about Bennett?"

"That's a whole other issue I haven't even thought about." The lie sours my mouth. Every time I tried to not think about him, I thought about him. And it didn't help that while I was in Colorado I found a cute family-owned woodworking shop. Everything inside reminded me of Bennett, including a similar truss table that he built.

"Have you talked to him?"

"No. He's left me numerous voicemails, but I couldn't bear to listen. Every time I heard his voice, all the hurt would come rushing back to me like a tidal wave. Everything that Jared did came rushing back and it hurt. I just don't know what to say. It was so hard to see all those women leaving messages for him on that stupid app."

"I know but I think he really cares about you. I'm sure there's a reasonable explanation for all of this. Trey says he's pretty sure Bennett loves you. When guys confess their feelings to other guys, that must mean they're true."

"Wait. When did you talk to Trey? And since when did you guys become close friends?"

"Oh, uh. Not the point." She reaches for my hand. "This is about you. Talk to Bennett. Hear him out."

My eyes wander to the second floor and then back to Olivia. "Has he come in yet?"

"I saw his car in the parking garage but never saw him come in. He must of came in early?" Olivia gives me a one shoulder shrug and swivels her chair to face her computer. My eyes dart to the second floor again and linger for a few seconds before turning my chair around to start my own work.

Throughout the morning I try to keep myself busy, but every time the elevator dings, my eye shift to see if it's Bennett. But each time I'm disappointed when it isn't. The afternoon light shines in through the skylight, catching my bottle of water and causing a prism of colors to shine across my desk. My eyes follow the light, while thoughts of everything except work flood my mind.

"Hi, Charlie." A familiar voice catches me off guard.

I look up and clutch my chest. "Hi, Liana. You startled me. Let me page Bennett for you." I reach for the phone, but she stops me.

"Actually, I'm here to see you. I was hoping we could talk. Do you have a lunch break?"

My eyebrows shoot up. Then I check the time. "Oh, yeah. Give me a few minutes."

Olivia gives me a quizzical look as she watches the entire interaction. I mouth that I'm going to lunch with Liana. As we exit the building, a cool nip in the air causes me to tug my over-sized cardigan closed. The fall breeze cooling my heated face. I tell Liana about a little bistro a short walk around the corner.

When we arrive, we're escorted to our seats with views overlooking the harbor, and the waiter passes us our menus. I browse the items on the menu, not really reading the words but needing anything to distract myself from the inevitable.

"So, how are you doing?" Liana asks.

I peer over my menu before placing it on the wrought iron tabletop. "I'm good. How are you? Mark and the kids?"

"Good. Everyone is good. To cut to the chase, I'm sure you know I'm not here for small talk."

Damn, that's what I was afraid of.

Liana continues. "I wanted to talk about Bennett being a dumbass."

The water I was drinking spews out of my mouth and all over the table. Quickly, I use my hand to shield from any other liquids that may fly out. "I'm so sorry. I wasn't expecting that."

She chuckles and hands me a napkin. "It's okay. I was a little blunt with that. But you see, Bennett hasn't been in a lot of relationships. At least serious ones. But he is the most loyal and faithful person I know. And I'm not saying that just because he's my brother. In fact, I would be the first person to call him out on his bullshit. So, I know he would never hurt you on purpose." She reaches over to cover my hand. "I have never seen him look at a girl like he looks at you. You've brought out a completely different side of him."

Just then, the waiter interrupts to take our order. This gives me a moment to absorb everything she said. Once our menus are cleared, she continues.

"Also, I am partially to blame, or at least my kids are."

I tilt my head. "What do you mean?"

"The night Bennett picked you up from Porter's, he was at my house and my kids were hounding him to play with his phone and they must have somehow got into the app and started sending random messages to people."

"Oh." I pause for a moment, needing to digest that information. "That could explain the messages, but why did he still have the app?"

"Because he's a dumbass." We both laugh. "I do know that he really cares for you and he's beating himself up about it. You really gotta talk to him."

I nod "I will. I just need a little more time."

A few moments later our food arrives. We spend the next thirty minutes eating and making small talk, but the whole time my thoughts are on Bennett and if Colorado is the right choice.

CHAPTER THIRTY-THREE

Expect the unexpected

Bennett

I bring the beer bottle up to my lips and take a swig as I flip through the channels on the television, nothing holding my attention. Just as I go to take another pull, my driveway alarm sounds. Odd. I'm not expecting anyone. Rising to my feet, I stride to the picture window and peel back the curtain. A Chevy Trailblazer comes to a stop in my driveway. After avoiding me for how long, *now* she's ready to talk.

Before she can even make it up the few steps, I'm opening the door. The setting sun creates a halo around her. Damn, she looks like an angel. Her long, pink dress is hugging her body in all the right places. A white cardigan is draped off one shoulder, showing off her sun-kissed tan skin. My dick twitches in my pants at the sight of her. *Simmer down, I don't think she's here for you.* I prop myself in the doorway, beer still in my hand. "What are you doing here?"

She looks down, gnawing on her bottom lip before returning her eyes to mine. "Do you have a few minutes to talk?"

Without a word, I step aside and motion for her to come

in. As she glides past, her sweet jasmine scent surrounds me. A scent I am so familiar with. One I can never smell without my thoughts going to her. Once inside, Charlie turns on her heel to face me.

"Liana came to talk to me today. She explained what happened." I open my mouth to speak, but she holds up a finger to stop me. "Just let me get this out." She paces back and forth, wringing her hands together. "When I caught my ex on that site, it messed with me. I may not have shown it, but it was always sitting in the back of my head. Would I be able to trust anyone again? Then when I thought I was over it, I saw you getting messages and it felt like the same thing all over again."

I grip her shoulders to stop her movements and look her in the eyes. "But it wasn't the same. I honestly thought I deleted the app. I never got any notifications because I wasn't sending messages to anyone. You're the only one I want."

"But in my head it was. It was Jared all over again. I really care for you, Bennett, but I need to do this for me. I think it's best if I take the job." Her gaze casts downward, then she starts to turn toward the door but stops and cocks her head to the side. "Is that the potholder I made?" She points to the coffee table in my living room.

I eye the phallus shaped knit potholder. "Yeah."

"Huh."

When she turns to face me, I grip her cheeks, resting my forehead on hers. "Charlie, I love you. I need you. I'm a shell of a man without you."

Tears prick her eyes. "I can't. Not right now." She takes a deep breath. "But we can be friends."

Dropping my hands, I take a step back. "Friends? I don't want to be friends." She flinches at my harsh tone. "I love you. I can't just be friends with you. Does that mean nothing to you?"

"That's not fair. Of course, it means something. It means

everything. I just… I'm sorry." She wipes a stray tear off her cheek. "I have to go."

With that, she yanks the door open and runs down the stairs, her dress flowing behind her as I watch from the doorway. She climbs into her SUV and starts the engine. A trail of red illuminates my driveway as she leaves. I stand there for a few minutes, everything and nothing running through my mind. The girl I can't live without just left, but I'm not ready to let her go. You only live once and if I can't do that with the one person I love, it's not worth living. I turn around and slam the door behind me.

The following day, I make my way to the elevator and press the button for the second floor. My feet carry me past my office and straight to the door at the end of the hall. When I reach the closed mahogany door, I lift my hand. I pause for a moment before I rap my knuckles on the wood. A moment later, it opens, and Frank is standing in front of me. He steps to the side to let me walk past him. I hear a soft click over my pounding heart as the door closes behind me.

CHAPTER THIRTY-FOUR

I want you

Charlie

I've been on auto pilot since talking to Bennett. The Blue Stone Group wanted me to move as soon as possible, so at the beginning of the week I collected boxes for all my belongings. They arranged a temporary apartment for me in Colorado, and a moving truck was scheduled to arrive in a couple of days. *This was what I wanted, right?* At least I thought it was.

Now I sit on the floor, cross-legged amongst stacks of cardboard boxes, some full and marked with a sharpie, others half empty. I bring the glass of Pinot Noir up to my lips, inhaling the rich fruit flavors with undertones of allspice. I take a sip of my wine, hoping the alcohol will calm my erratic nerves. Nope, it doesn't. I just pray that I haven't made a giant mistake.

A booming knock on my front door, has me jumping, and spilling my wine. Shit. I yank off my sock and swipe at the liquid before it stains the hardwood floor.

"Charlie! Open up!" Another loud knock follows.

"Bennett?" My brows knit together as I turn the handle to open the door.

Bennett comes crashing through the doorway. His gaze darts around the room, taking in all the boxes before his eyes stop on me. His chest rising and falling like he just ran a marathon. He stalks towards me and in three giant steps, he's toe to toe with me. His hands clasp my face, and his lips are on mine. My hands reach up to clasp onto his forearms like he's my lifeline. There's nothing tender about the kiss. His lips are firm and demanding. It's a kiss with a purpose. When he pulls away slightly, my eyes flutter open and gaze into his blue orbs.

"Charlie Jean Hansley. I love you. I've loved you since the first time I saw you. My life is empty without you in it." He brushes a loose strand of hair behind my ear. "So that's why I'm here. I can't let you go just yet."

My heart feels like it's going to beat out of my chest. I hold my breath as I wait for what he's going to say next. I just want him to tell me he wants me to stay. His eyes dart between mine and what feels like minutes have only been seconds.

"I quit my job. I want to come with you to Colorado."

I blink. And blink again, trying to understand the words that just came out of his mouth. He quit his job. For me. A giggle escapes my lips, followed by a full on belly laugh. Bennett pulls away, his eyebrows knit together.

"Well, that wasn't the answer I was expecting."

Still doubled over from laughter, inhaling deeply to catch my breath, I wipe the tears from my eyes and look at Bennett, confusion all over his face. I grab his hand.

"I don't know what to say. You quit your job for me. A job you're so good at and love. But you might get kinda lonely out in Colorado."

His eyebrow quirks up. "What do you mean?"

"I told HR today that I couldn't take the job. I'm not moving."

His eyes light up and a dazzling smile spreads across his

face. He wraps his arms around my waist and picks me up and twirls me around. Setting me back down to my feet, he looks into my eyes.

"I love you."

"I love you too, Bennett."

His lips are back on mine. This time softer, more sensual. My hands reach up to wrap around his neck, but he pulls away.

"Why'd you decide to stay?"

I squeeze my eyes shut before I open one to look at Bennett. My hands fly up to cover my heated face, muffling my voice. "Because of the penis potholder." When I dare to look at him again, I continue. "You kept something that I gave you that's so ugly and looks like a penis." He grabs my hands and intertwines his fingers with mine and bends his knees so he's at eye level with me, his look encouraging me to continue. "And what guy keeps penis shaped objects. But you kept it and something about that told me I was making a huge mistake if I left you."

"It was from you. Of course, I was going to keep it."

This time, I rise to my toes and kiss him. Without missing a beat, Bennett takes over. His tongue caresses the seam of my lips and I open to give him access, our tongues swirling against one another. His hands skims down my back until he reaches my butt cheeks and then he lifts me. My legs instinctively wrap around his waist. He walks until my back hits the first solid surface. He uses the wall to help keep me propped up as he grinds into me. His jeans rub against my cotton shorts. I release a moan as the friction against my clit becomes too much. His hard cock rubbing in the right spot each time he moves his hips.

Bennett breaks away from our kiss. Desire swarms his hooded eyes. "I love you so fucking much."

"I love you, too. But right now, I need you inside of me."

Bennett fumbles as he tries to unbutton his pants with one hand. My hands move to the hem of my shirt and tug up. Halfway over my head, my arm gets stuck, and my nose is blocking the collar from my shirt coming completely off.

"This isn't working," Bennett mumbles.

I let out a squeal as he picks me up. With one eye, I watch as he carries me to the kitchen counter a few steps away. His arms swiftly sweeps over the top, knocking over a pile of papers and a mug that shatters to the ground. He helps me untangle my shirt and flings it over his head. "Sorry about the mug. I'll buy you a new one."

"No worries. I have plenty." My hands thread to his hair as I bring his lips to mine. I kiss him with fervor, reaching down to stroke his thickening cock through his jeans.

"Oh fuck, Charlie. I need you," he gasps out.

"I'm right here." This time I reach to undo the button and tug his pants and boxer briefs down. My slender fingers wrap around his thick shaft, barely touching as I stroke him up and down. When I reach the tip, I squeeze and twist. A deep moan rumbled from Bennett's throat. His head falls back in ecstasy as his hips pump erratically in my hand.

Bennett's gaze drifts downwards to where I'm stroking him and then returns to me. "Fuck. Your fingers wrapped around me feels so fucking good, but if we don't stop, I'm going to shoot my load all over your stomach." He takes a step forward causing me to lose my grip on his cock. His hands clasp my cheeks, forcing me to look up at him. "My turn." Bennett reaches around, unclasping my bra and dragging the straps down my arms. He drops it on the floor as his eyes take in my naked chest. He reaches up to cup my right breast, his thumb brushing over my hard nipple. I arch my back, pressing my breast into his hand, loving the way his hands feel on my body. His other hand inches its way up my thigh until his fingers reach the hem of my shorts and he tugs. "These need to go."

I hook my thumbs into the waistband of my shorts and shimmy them down my thighs until they fall to the floor. Bennett grabs my knees and spreads me open. He takes a step forward, his thick cock brushing against my clit. He dips his hand between us, and his fingers spread me open and swirls my moisture around. Then he plunges his finger into me.

"Oh, that feels so good." I moan. I lean back on my hands to give him more room between us.

He thrusts a few more times before inserting another digit, stretching me even more. I rock my hips, mimicking his motion. He inserts another finger as he pinches my nipple. Another moan escapes my lips. I watch his lust filled gaze as he moves his fingers in and out.

"Ah yes. Please. I need more." I pant.

His eyes trail up my body until they meet mine. His fingers still fucking me harder with each thrust, twisting when he pulls out and pushes back in. "What do you want?"

"I want you."

"But what do you need?"

My hands fly to his shoulders, my nails digging into his flesh in frustration. "I need your cock inside me, fucking me. Now!"

"I like it when you get all demanding." He pulls his fingers out of me. The loss of him causes me to whimper. He brings his fingers up to his mouth and sucks my arousal off each digit. A deep moan comes from his throat as he releases my fingers with a pop.

"Fuck. You taste delicious."

"Well, you can finish that meal later. Just fuck me already."

He releases a laugh. His eyes dart downward, then back up to mine. "Dammit. I don't have a condom." His eyes close. Disappointment crosses his face.

"Mine are in a box somewhere over there." I point behind me. "I'm on the pill if you want to go without."

"Are you sure?"

I nod. His lips press to mine as he drags me to the edge of the counter. The tip of his cock teases my entrance before he presses all the way in.

He starts with slow, shallow thrusts. "Feeling how your body grips my dick feels fan-fucking-tastic."

"Oh, yes." I moan. My heels dig into his ass, encouraging him to move faster. Understanding my need, he picks up his pace. One of my hands grips his shoulder and the other clenches the hair on the back of his head. He dips as he takes a hard nipple in his mouth. He sucks and swirls his tongue around my stiff peak, then bites down, sending a jolt of pleasure through my body.

Bennett grabs my ankles and moves them, so my feet are on the counter, spreading my legs open further. I lean back on my hands, he grips my knees as he continues to pound into me, each thrust harder and deeper than the last. His hand goes to my aching clit, rubbing it in tandem as he pumps in and out of me.

"Oh God, Bennett. I'm going to come." I pant, feeling the build start in my core. Bennett's thrusts become more erratic. His grunts mix with my moans.

"Fuuuuck." Bennett's movements slow as his release spills into me. He works on collecting his breath as I do the same. His hands cage my face, and his soft lips caress my own. "God, you're perfect," he whispers before placing another kiss on my lips. He slowly pulls out. "Let me clean you up." His eyes scan the kitchen for anything he could use when he snags a roll of paper towels from a box.

When he's finished cleaning us up, he pulls up his boxer briefs and tugs his shirt over my head. I rest my head on his shoulder. "I can't believe you quit your job."

"I can't believe you're staying. That could have ended in disaster." He lets out a chuckle, rubbing his hands slowly up and down my back.

Lifting my head, I look him in the eyes. "What are you going to do? Are you going to ask for your job back?"

"Actually, I've been thinking I might turn my woodworking into a business. I already have a list of loyal customers and not working a nine to five will give me more time to devote to working in my shop."

"Really? That would be amazing. Your work is so beautiful."

"Yeah, my sister has always been telling me to start my own business. Then with your encouragement, I thought, why not. Don't get me wrong, I enjoy my job. It's provided me with the security I always wanted for my family. But now it's time I start making decisions for myself. Go after the things I want and one of those things is you."

A tear forms in the corner of my eye and then falls down my cheek. Followed by another on the opposite side.

"Hey, why the tears?" He brushes his thumb to wipe away the moisture.

"This is going to sound so stupid." My hands go up to cover my face, a tremble in my voice.

"Nothing is stupid," he reassures me.

"I've never had someone give up so much for me. To love me so much they're willing to sacrifice so much."

"I would sacrifice the world for you. I would even sacrifice my Hot Wheels collection for you."

His lips turn to a smile when I slap his chest.

"Oh, that's serious talk there."

"It would be hard. Tears might be shed, but totally worth it." He reaches for my hand and intertwines our fingers bringing it up to his lips, placing kisses on my palm and wrist.

I turn my head and look at all the boxes. "Guess I'll be spending my weekend unpacking all these."

"Or we could finish packing everything and bring it all to my house."

My head shoots back to Bennett.

"Are you asking me to move in with you?"

"Well, I didn't ask, but it beats unpacking it all just to repack it later." He winks.

EPILOGUE

Two months later

Charlie

"Everyone, raise your glass. Congratulations Charlie!" Olivia shouts over the noise at Porter's. "Here's to your last day at The Blue Stone Group. The chair next to me will forever be empty without you."

The clinking of glasses and bottles echoes around our table along with a collective cheer.

"Thanks everyone. It's going to be so weird not seeing everyone Monday morning anymore." I glance around the table at the smiling faces of my friends. Most importantly, who knew I would fall in love with the man I loathed for so many months.

"I'm sure they'll give you your job back," Parisa says.

"What will you do with all your time now?" Seth asks at the same time.

Bennett wraps his arm around my waist and pulls me close. "Don't worry guys, I'll keep my little sex kitten busy." He winks. Bennett's furniture business has gained popularity, so I've come on to help him run his business. As for the nickname, he still hasn't let that one go.

"Oh yeah. I'm sure you'll keep her plenty busy." Trey waggles his eyebrows. Olivia smacks him on the arm.

"And I have these!" I reach down into my bag and set a white box imprinted with The Sweet Spot logo on the table. "This will be my last Friday cupcake day, so I had to get them." I flip open the box showcasing the salted caramel cupcakes with coconut brittle.

Parisa peers into the box. "These aren't plain vanilla with a buttercream frosting." She eyes me suspiciously.

I shrug a shoulder. "It was time for something different. Something unpredictable." A smile graces my face as I wrap my arms around Bennett's waist. Instinctively, his arm wraps around my shoulder and he places a quick kiss on my forehead.

With me and Bennett at the head of the table, Trey and Olivia are to our right with Seth and Parisa to our left. Bennett is talking animatedly with Trey when his hand swipes across the table, sending my clutch to the floor.

"Oh sorry, let me get that." Bennett is about to stand when I tell him I got it.

I push my chair away from the table and crouch down to grab my clutch when movement under the table catches my eye. It takes a moment for my eyes to adjust, then it dawns on me, it's Seth's hand rubbing up and down Parisa's thigh. Hurrying back up to my seat, I set my clutch on the table. My gaze darts to Seth and then to Parisa. Both are concentrated on what Trey is talking about and not caring what is happening under the table.

Without notice, Parisa stands from her chair. "It's been fun everyone. I have a few things at home I need to get done so I'm going to call it a night." When she moves to collect her bag her hand brushes across Seth's shoulder, and he looks up giving her a shy smile. I stand along with Olivia to give Parisa a hug.

Seth stands from his seat as well. "Yeah. I'm going to head out too. I've got some things to do."

Trey covers his mouth with his fist, faking a cough while he says, "Or someone."

Seeming to be the only one who heard him, I narrow my eyes at Trey. When his gaze meets mine, a dazzling grin covers his face.

We watch in fascination as Parisa, and Seth walk towards the exit together. As soon as they're out of sight, I turn to Trey. "What do you know?"

Trey lets out a deep laugh. "I told you we'll see who gets the last laugh." He points to Bennett and then leans in, and everyone follows suit. "Listen to this…"

The End

Thank you so much for reading Flirting with the Playboy! If you want more Charlie and Bennett here is a BONUS SCENE for newsletter subscribers. Scan for exclusive access.

Coming fall of 2022, the next book in the Harbor Highlands Series, Flirting with the Enemy! Parisa and Seth's Story.

All is fair in love and promotions.

Pre-order now!

Acknowledgments

First and foremost, I want to thank everyone who picked up this book. I think I will forever be in awe that someone wants to read my stories.

I have to thank my husband. I don't know if I would have ever started writing and publishing journey without his words of encouragement. A big shout out to Brandi Zelenka. You were there for me every step of the way and I don't think I could have done this without you.

To my creative team, you pushed me to put out the best book possible and I am so thankful to have you on my side. Thank you to my editor, Brandi at My Notes in the Margin. I tend to give you a hot mess and you make it brilliant. Thank you so my beta readers, Ashley Cestra and Breanna Harkins. You gave me invaluable feedback to help make my manuscript sparkle. And Teagan Reichuber, thank you for your last minutes eyes on this book. You helped me out so much. Jessica Hollyfield and Kristi Webster, both of you are fantastic cheerleaders and I am so honored to have you both in my corner and answer all my oddball questions. Meghan Quinn, thank you for all your amazing advice.

Thank you Ena at Enticing Journey Book Promotions for helping out a brand new author. You made everything run smoothly. Thank you to all the bloggers, bookstagrammers, and booktokers for reading and sharing your excitement for this book. It means the world to me and I can't thank you enough.

I hope to see you at the next book!

Other titles by Gia Stevens

Harbor Highlands Series

About the Author

Gia Stevens resides in the *up north* of Minnesota. She lives for the warm, sunny days of summer and dreads the bitter cold of winter. A romantic comedy junkie at heart, she knew she wanted her own stories to encompass those same feelings.

When she's not busy writing your next book boyfriend, Gia can be found playing in her vegetable garden, watching reruns of The OC and Gossip Girl, or curled up with a good book.

Visit my website for more information.
https://authorgiastevens.com